unholy COMMUNION

unholy COMMUNION

LAQUISHA HALL

purposely created
PUBLISHING

dedication

To every person who shared their story with me
and whose life has been affected by sexual abuse.

You are not alone.

table of contents

acknowledgements

Without the support of family, my "extended family" and dear friends, I would never have mustered the strength to finish this book.

I am thankful to all advocacy organizations and advocates who have supported me and allowed me to support them over the years.

Sisters for Sisters, Inc., the Black Doll Affair, Heal a Woman to Heal a Nation, Inc. and Stop the Silence, Inc., thank you for your support over the years.

To Joan Hall-Hovey, my Winghill Online Writing Coach, for tirelessly sending me feedback and direction.

To my initial editor, Rachel Wallach, thank you for taking on this task with such excitement and patience.

To those who inspired and pushed me to write the vision out and sit down and finish this book, thank you.

Tieshena Davis, Founder of Purposely Created Publishing, thank you for helping me push this baby out and kicking my butt when I didn't want to!

Mothyna James-Brightful, I will never forget that "self love is not selfish."

Pastor Daniel and First Lady Tonya Spellman and Guiding Light Apostolic Church in Camden, North Carolina, thank you for taking me in when I felt put out.

Pastors Joel and Freda Anderson and Open Door Fellowship Church in Randallstown, Maryland, thank you for allowing me to join a group who is *loving genuinely and inspiring hope.*

I emphatically give a special thank you to my wonderful, compassionate and accommodating husband, Mardis C. Hall, who allowed me to see that there are great men who walk among us.

author's note

Sexual abuse is a serious crime. According to Allaboutcounseling.com, one in three girls and one in five boys are sexually abused before the age of eighteen. This crime can be viewed as even more heinous because of the identities of the abusers. A person would like to think that the persons committing these crimes are criminals on the streets, the common rapist or volatile stranger. However, the most common pedophiles are those persons that children look up to and trust, more specifically and commonly, a family member or person living within the family household.

There is a joint "crime" in addition to the sexual abuse that is rarely discussed: the crime of the adults or parents who do not invite their children to trust them or confide in them.

According to Susan Forward, Ph.D., the author of *Innocence and Betrayal Overcoming the Legacy of Sexual Abuse*, ninety percent of sexual abuse victims never tell*. Some children do not tell because the pedophile has convinced them that the activities between them is their "little secret," and some do not tell because of the relationship or bond the pedophile holds with the person they would tell.

Allaboutcounseling.com states, "Mothers have conflicting allegiances; they love their children and their mate. It's hard to believe that someone they love could commit such a monstrous act, particularly on their own child. It can become very traumatic and chaotic to families dealing with this issue." However, this is disheartening and too much of a burden for a young person to carry. This is also an emotional devastation to the victim since they are the one who will recall horrific thoughts throughout their lifetime.

Some adults are in denial: "This would not happen to my child." Because they are naïve and innocent, any young person is vulnerable to sexual abuse. Some victims are in denial: "This is not what is happening to me. We love each other." Any sexual relationship between an adult and a child is not an act of love. Usually, victims from dysfunctional families or victims who have a poor relationship with their parents are those who seek "love" in the wrong places. This "love" could commonly be formed between a victim and their pedophile.

My advice to **sexual abuse victims** is to tell—know that the abuse is not your fault and believe in being victorious in spite of catastrophe. First, Allaboutcounseling.com reminds victims that "a late report is earlier than never." Even if the person you tell is a school friend, who would in turn probably have no clue what to do for you, tell somebody. Relief is found when you get problematic circumstances off of your chest. In addition, you never know who would be willing to help if you do not say something to someone.

Second, do not allow yourself to believe that you can control an adult's actions. An adult is supposed to train or teach you, not vice versa. Not one ounce of the sexual abuse could have been caused or initiated by you. If you were seeking love and accepted the abuse, you are still not at fault. The "adult" should have shown you a different version of "love."

Finally, it is very easy to become discouraged and depressed as a victim of sexual abuse. However, you must realize that you can still become a lawyer for one of the nation's largest law firms, like Cupcake Brown, or simply a teacher, like me, who can help influence other youth who may be encountering similar situations. Do not give up on yourself because of the dirty mind of your attacker!

My advice to **parents of sexual abuse victims** is to always be a support to your child, which would equate to never allowing a door to be closed to communication, and investigate any accusations. "Often times, long term trauma results not from the abuse itself, but from the lack of support, belief or attention to pain. This can intensify or prolong trauma from abuse," states Allaboutcounseling.com.

First, a parent can close the door to communication by dishing out constant verbal abuse to a child or by simply keeping their bedroom door closed, which would not enable the child to feel free to come to the parent. By being a support, your child will not be afraid to approach you. The child will be less likely to discuss any private matters with you if you are constantly showing disgust or anger with your child. This is not only important because of sexual abuse, but also in cases where your child may encounter other dangerous situations, for example, smoking or the loss of virginity. The support of a parent will embrace an even closer relationship with the child when the child becomes an adult.

Second, it does not matter if you believe you have birthed the child who cried wolf; if your child, whom you love, comes to you and says someone inappropriately touched them, investigate. Don't show your doubts to your child initially, but rather show care, concern and love. Privately investigate if you are not sure. You will be satisfied to know that you found out for yourself after being told instead of being tormented for years with the thought, "what if it did happen?"

❖ ❖ ❖

The genre of this novel is labeled "fiction," but the events are true for many youth. This novel is based on events that occurred in my life. The pastor who molested me is still roaming our world, still a pastor... and possibly, still a pedophile.

PART 1

"We are troubled on every side, yet not distressed; we are perplexed, but not in despair;

Persecuted, but not forsaken; cast down, but not destroyed"

Aliyana

"Hey! Get up!" My mother is louder than a warmed up fire truck. This is what I wake up to every school day. It is time to go to school and get out of this place I am forced to call home.

In my mind, I wrestle with whether I would rather stay home or go to school. It is hard to get out of bed. Besides the fact that it is cold inside and outside of the house, I am not going to want to remake my Sesame Street-themed bed (my mother chose these childish sheets!). I do like school, but I do not love it. I hate getting up at 5 every weekday morning just to sit through five 90-minute classes. I do get to see my friends when I go, people who understand me and people that I call my family. Some of my classes are interesting, especially art, Japanese I and English, but I also have classes I abhor, like math. Anyways, I sometimes feel that anything is better than staying cooped up in my small house, where I only feel loved by my younger sisters, Layne and Anne.

My dad, even though he does not live with us anymore, shows that he loves me by fighting for visitation rights continually, even though my mother tries her best to deter him. My mother—well, she birthed me. Currently, she is showing her love by keeping food on the table (I have to ask for something to drink), clothes on my back (I am 14, and she is still picking out my clothes) and shelter over my head (where I share a room with my nocturnally urinating sister). I am grateful for these material things, but it's feelings that I want: love, from a mother to her daughter.

"Get up now!"

I need to get dressed and stop daydreaming. I have to "wash up," which entails using a bar of soap and a rag in a small basin of water. My mother said too much water is used in a shower. As a result, I am only allowed to either wash up or take a bath in the tub, which I have to also share with my sisters. Taking a shower in our household is equivalent to having sex or skipping church: forbidden. While washing up and getting dressed, I hear the local news station's theme music, the same melody that I hear every morning— so annoying, but so familiar.

Every day, before I leave for school, I have to go before the court and be found innocent or guilty as far as what I have chosen to wear. The judge will either condemn me and make me change my clothes, or send me on my way. So here I go again, another day of trying to prove myself. I knock on the judge's door.

"Ma? Hey, Ma?" I am so nervous, but for what?

"Wha' chu' want?" The judge is irritable already at 5:45 a.m.

"Don't you have to look at my clothes?" She knows why I am knocking on her door. But all I hear for at least 30 seconds is silence. Why does she do this to me? Is it to preserve her authority? A mind game?

"Open da door."

I walk into her bedroom. The bedside lamp sheds a very low light. My mother sits in her queen-size bed, with her head resting on her arm and a Bible under her face. What a joke. She is far from God-fearing, which she shows by cussing me out every other day. My mother has the facial features of an Indian. Her attractively pronounced cheekbones sit beneath a pair of almond-shaped, dark eyes. Her usually tamed hair is currently wild from sleep. Her hair is thick, sitting just above her shoulders with wool-like ends. My mother is naturally beautiful but currently looks groggy and tired. I look at her and wonder why I cannot talk to her. Why can't we just have a decent conversation without her yelling or cussing at me? Why is it that every time I try to please her, be nice, be a loving daughter, I fail? Briefly, I begin to daydream a beautiful mother-daughter relationship. I walk into her room, slip into her bed and watch the TV with her while we share our thoughts about the upcoming day. I picture a daughter who pulls her mom's hair back and whispers in her ear while the mom lets out a giggle. The daughter then reaches for her mom's neck. Her mom embraces her in a warm hug.

"Fix yourself up! Why you look so crazy? Tuck that shirt in." I am 110 pounds. I wear a size 0-1 in bottoms and a small in tops. I am standing before my mother in an oversized, small (according to the Super 10 discount store), cotton jersey like button up shirt with thick white and orange vertical stripes and a pair of white, baggy jeans. My new shoes, advertised all summer for $9.99 at Payless, are cream-colored canvas. I knew that I could not get a pair of expensive shoes, so I settled for these when my mother took me to the store. This outfit, chosen by my mother, makes me look sloppy even when I try not to.

"Why are you standing there looking stupid?" my mother asks.

If I look stupid, I am wearing the clothes you picked for me, so...

"I'm not—"

"All right then, get out!"

With my hair braided in two jumbo cornrows, I slowly back out of the room, attempting to keep my composure. I recall sitting on the floor last night while my mother braided my hair thinking that I would be teased unmercifully by my peers for these cornrows. Most of my friends got braids or a perm over the summer in preparation for the beginning of the new school year. Where do I think I am going with my *The Color Purple* original hairstyle?

I cannot help but wonder why I have to go through this embarrassing routine with my mother daily. What did I do to deserve this treatment from her? She has an unstated hatred for me for unknown reasons. I know this from the grimaces she gives me when she thinks I am not looking, from her constant name-calling (calling me a female dog is her favorite) and because she will not allow me to hug or kiss her—or even touch her, for that matter.

All I want is her unconditional love.

I grab a bowl of corn flakes with ten spoonfuls of sugar and then run outside to wait for the school bus. I am bothered by a fear: If my mother talks about how badly I look, what will my peers say?

Sadie Mae

I sleep off and on throughout the night. Why? My ex-husband and respected city police officer, Richard, used to beat me like I was a man. I guess I am just nervous—nervous that Richard may disturb my home (again) in the middle of the night. Since my sleep is already broken into sections, it is easy for me to be the alarm clock for the kids.

"Get up now!" I yell a final time at my oldest child. I don't know what is taking her so long, but she better act like she knows. She already takes too long in the bathroom. I sure do believe that all she does is go in the bathroom and run a lot of water that she doesn't use anyway since she comes out still musty sometimes.

As soon as I start to drift off to sleep again, here she comes knocking at my door, "Ma? Hey, Ma?"

"Wha' chu want?" I yell, not wanting to be bothered.

"Don't you have to look at my clothes?"

I bet she has the most stupid look on her face right now. Sometimes I wonder where my first child came from.

"Open da door," I scream as I stop myself from cursing, a bad habit that I just cannot seem to break since the divorce. Here she comes walking in my bedroom, looking retarded.

"Fix yourself up! Why you look so crazy? Tuck that shirt in." It is such a hard job for a mother to ensure that her children go to school dressed appropriately.

"I can't, it's too long and... because—"

"I didn't ask you what you can't do! I told you to do it!" I scream again.

I am watching her do what I ask, speedily. But now I want her out of my face. She looks just like her no-good daddy, who impregnated me with her when I was 17 years old as a result of my refusal to listen to my mother; now, she will not listen to me, which is probably why we don't have such a great relationship as a mother and daughter. She constantly sits in her room and talks about how she wishes she lived with my sister and her two children "because they have their own room and their momma doesn't call them names." Every time I turn around she is talking about how she can't wait to see Richard. She even sneaks and calls him from my mother's phone. I don't know why she sides with that bastard. Besides, he ain't paying no child support anyway. I look at her in disgust just thinking about it.

"Why are you standing there looking stupid?"

"I'm not—"

"All right then, get out!"

I read another verse of my Bible: "Weeping may endure for a night, but joy comes in the morning." I go back to sleep.

The Pastor

I open my eyes to dimmed sunlight. I know that I need to get out of my bed and say my prayers, especially with the dream I had last night! But I don't feel like it. So with my eyes closed, I simply say my prayers in my mind. This seems to be ineffective since I am reliving my dream. A church member comes to my study for counseling and brings along her young daughter. The woman willingly steps aside, yapping away about her problem, while I pull up the young girl's skirt to reveal the smooth and fruity scent of flesh. I slide her panties down, which have the day of the week embroidered across the back: Sunday. I lead her into the main sanctuary, and she bends over on a pew. A young, virginal body for me to seduce over and over, anytime I desire, without interference from her mother.

"Thank you, Lord," I say aloud. But sometimes I wonder if I really mean what I say when I thank God. Do I really believe that God even hears my cries for strength and protection with the lustful thoughts I so frequently entertain? All I know is that I better mean it because I have to preach tonight.

I am the pastor of Cyprian Baptist Church. I came to this church about a year ago. The congregation received me well. I really believe that they enjoy my preaching, especially when I stomp my feet hard in conjunction with my heavy breathing and pauses between every five words or so. I get into the services so much that sometimes I feel like I am the one who created the pre-written sermons. Yes, God is good.

As I walk down the hall to the bathroom, I think about Sadie Mae. She will be calling me in about 20 minutes or so. My second cousin, Sadie, with her fine self, has been a desire of my heart since we were children. It is possible that since our mothers got together so frequently that we may have spent a little too much time together growing up. As children, we were made to take naps on and under large blankets laid on the floor. However, this simply turned into a kissing cousins session for us. It would thrill me just to lie beside her. I always felt like I was with my very own Pocahontas. Even as a child, I thought Sadie Mae was so pretty, with her almond-shaped eyes, sun-kissed fair skin and nearly bone straight long hair. It was all I needed to watch as I fell asleep. I kissed her everywhere that I found to be beautiful: her eyes, her nose, her forehead, her cheeks and her lips, which is where she would recoil in disgust, but allowed me to continue. The scent of soap and the warmth of her body are what caused me to feel my first erection at 13 years old. She would still allow me to kiss her in all the same places I kissed as a child, but this time I was allowed to use my finger inside her underwear, which was a simple exploration activity for both of us. Even though we are now together as adults and have formed a relationship, I still wish we could be more. Husband and wife would be ideal but not feasible with her crazy family. Oh—it would be our crazy family, huh? I am only her second cousin, a distant relative, however, those country cows would never understand. They keep calling "incest" what I call pure enjoyment and pleasure.

Back to Sadie Mae. Usually when I visit her, I go to her house on a Monday and return back to my town that Wednesday. I will eagerly travel those two and a half hours from Fayetteville to New Bern just to get a taste of my Sadie. But don't get me wrong—I only desire a drop.

Sadie Mae is a shoe saleswoman for J.C. Penney. I don't know why she even works there because she comes home, calls me, and complains about it every day. I guess this is the type of thing that happens when a person does not graduate from college. I bless the name of the Lord for my doctorate in theology.

After I finish washing up, I contemplate which sermon I plan to use today at the guest church. I figure since it's a youth service, I guess I should preach about the youth of today...

The youth need to learn to obey their parents and their teachers...

And their faithful pastor.

The youth of today need to stop being fast: these little boys need to stop playing with the little girls' heads, and these little girls need to stop lying down with any kind of boy, getting pregnant at early ages...

Unless they lay down with a real man like me.

I realize I cannot focus my thoughts on what I should preach, so I decide to just refer to my pre-written sermons. One thing I know for sure is that the youth of today need the help of our Lord Jesus.

Aliyana

As much as I hate my outfit today, I really pretend well, in front of my friends, to be confident. I am sitting in the cafeteria with my friends, who are a good mixture of black, white, Filipino and Asian. We are all listening to our Walkmans, waiting for Michael Jackson's new song to play on the radio. "You Are Not Alone" was a big hit with my crowd because of its romantic and melodic background music, or simply because it was Michael.

"I am about to call the station and tell them to play our song. Aliyana, you got 35 cent for da call?" asks one friend.

"Do I look like I got any money?"

Another student, who is sitting nearby and who I do not usually associate myself with, says, "If you did have some money you need to use it to get a toothbrush and some toothpaste!"

The entire table, except one person, bursts out laughing. Helena, my one loyal friend, responds, "Why don't you shut up, with your permanently bloated tail, looking like a whale outside of water!"

I grin, not because my friend had a comeback to defend me, but because I was fighting back tears. Ever since I have had teeth, there has been something wrong with them. They protrude from my mouth, and my front two teeth have chocolate brown spots. I try to brush them off, scrub them off, and even scrape them off with a razor blade. As much as I brush, I should have the cleanest teeth in this school. But no matter how hard I try to hide the stains, they keep looking back at me in the mirror, mocking me every time I open my mouth.

I have been teased about my teeth ever since I started school. And in addition to what seems to be a permanently dirty mouth, I have jacked up clothes and a mother who couldn't care less.

The lunch bell rings. It is time for my choir class, a class where I have to open my mouth, again. And again.

And again.

Sadie Mae

I think back to last night, when I soaked my feet. Epsom salt and hot water seem to work wonders. Why think about this right now? I have only been at work for three and a half hours, and my feet are already screaming in pain. Here I am recommending to customers the most comfortable, "sole-saving" shoes, and my own feet are not saved. Albeit, I am wearing pumps.

Pumps with at least a three-inch heel not only make my legs, and more specifically my calf muscles, look good but also my outfits. My co-worker, Gayle, is always talking to me about my clothes.

"I just don't understand it, Sadie," Gayle says, "why you keep on comin' to work lookin' like dat, like you goin' to church or somethin'."

"You don't have to understand it," I reply, almost whispering, not wanting the customers to overhear her confrontation. I have an image to display, one of grace and elegance, as a lady, and I refuse to allow this slob to screw that up for me.

Today I am wearing a two-piece canary yellow suit with sequins and pearl buttons. I have a bag in my locker that matches my pearl colored pumps, which I have so perfectly matched with the buttons. What is wrong with looking this darn good?

"We are only selling shoes, and we only work at J.C. Penney. If you ask me, you are only showin' off," says Gayle.

"You know what—I didn't ask you, okay? And what I wear is none of your business. I don't have to take this!" I exclaim as I hurry to the break room in the back of the store. I can hear a customer ask Gayle if I am still going to help her find a pair of shoes, but I will not slow up to hear Gayle's reply.

C. J. told me that these women I work with are jealous of me. He said I have a Coca-Cola bottle figure, which I adorn with beautiful clothes, and I always keep my hair neatly pulled back into a ponytail if it is not curled. Gayle keeps coming to work looking busted and disgusted, with her Salvation Army flower print tops and regular slacks that are always black, white, or navy. She tries to curl her own hair, but it always turns out dry and frizzy. Her dark and uneven complexion is no match for my fair-skinned and even tone. With my naturally arched eyebrows, long lashes, and red lipstick-glazed lips, she should be jealous. The least she can do is put on a little makeup.

I will call C.J. as soon as I get in because I need to have my soul saved tonight.

The Pastor

Sitting in my office at the church is so relaxing. In this room there are mahogany and glass cabinets, an executive-size desk, and plaques, certificates, and degrees that line every bright white wall. A small window sits high up to my left, allowing the sunlight to dance across my closed eyelids.

"Umm, Pastor C.J. Whitaker?" asks one of my deacons.

"Yes!" I reply, trying to sound as if I am not about to fall asleep.

"Bishop Nelson at Trinity Baptist is on the phone trying to see if you are definitely coming."

"I'll take it," I say, and take my time raising myself in my chocolate brown leather desk chair.

"Pastor Whit—"

"Pastor Whitaker! Bless the name of the Lord! I am so excited to have you as our guest speaker tonight. Ya know everybody is comin' cause of you. Boy, you got a gift, a gift from—"

"Well, praise the Lord, Bishop."

"Yeah, praise Him! He is truly worthy. We are so happy and blessed to have such a dynamic speak—"

"OK, I will see you between 7 and 7:30 sharp," I say, rubbing my forehead.

"Thank you, thank you, Pastor. I am truly honored to—"

"I am sorry Bishop, but I've got a meeting," I reply, looking at my watch.

"Oh, I apologize for keeping you. But you know we will have a little paper in it for you."

"How much?" I ask, more willing to talk now.

"Well, you know we've gotta collect the offering first. Then we'll take up a speaker's off—"

"So basically, you're not sure, right?

"Well, I will find out for sure right now. Hold on..."

This Bishop is working my patience. He already interrupted my nap. I am giving up my Friday night for his church, too, so he better not try to give me no 100 dollar offering. At least 200.

"Pastor Whitaker?"

"Yes sir?"

"Three hundred all right? Whatever the saints don't give, well... I will make up the difference."

"That's fine, sir. Whatever the Lord gives, so shall it be," I say, rubbing my chin in satisfaction.

"Yes sir! Yes sir!" Bishop Nelson says with excitement as we both chuckle nervously.

"Well, we will be praying for your safe arrival, Pastor. Thank God for you and how you will bless the souls of our young people tonight! God knows that—"

"Bishop, I'm sorry. I have a meeting."

"Right, right, sir."

"Have a blessed day now."

"You too, praise God."

"All right," I say, glad to be able to finally hang up on his loquacious self. I sit back in my desk chair and wonder how long his Sunday services are.

I close my eyes again, in another attempt to conjure up a sermon for tonight. But my mind can't help but wonder if the young ladies will show up tonight dressed like they were the last time I preached at Bishop Nelson's church: half-dressed, no stockings, high, strappy heels, short skirts, peeking belly buttons, long weaves, low tops, lots of cleavage, and heavy makeup. Praise the Lord...

After I ask my assistant to lock and close my office door, I retrieve my bottle of lotion from my desk drawer and unzip my designer pants.

Aliyana

I have been singing in school choirs since middle school. Nothing has really changed as far as the format, except for in middle school, the choir sang with the band, as well as other presenters. In high school, Mrs. O's choir performs the entire concert.

Mrs. O is one of the most serious high school teachers I have ever had. Her real name is Mrs. Octavionrino, and she actually stresses over whether or not our choir is on pitch. A graduate from a professional music school, she has dreams of taking our choir to another level.

"We will have our annual Fall Concert in approximately one month!" Mrs. O exclaims. "Which means I will need your full attention and dedication to singing."

Students begin to murmur all over the room and then yell out questions.

"What will we be singing?"

"What will we wear?"

"Will the Show Troupe be invited?"

"Q-u-i-e-t! This is not the time for you to begin talking but for you to work!" Mrs. O shouts. Next up, the impudent student.

"If Show Troupe is gonna be in da concert then I don' wanna sing."

Silence blanketed the classroom, and students with rotating heads glance back and forth from the student to Mrs. O.

"What exactly is that supposed to mean?" asks Mrs. O.

Mrs. O knows exactly what that comment means and where it comes from. Show Troupe is the new choir recently founded by Mrs. O. In order to escape the common choir sounds of bass, tenor, alto and soprano, Mrs. O held tryouts to form a girls' choir. She auditioned many, but only accepted nine.

The difference between Show Troupe and a traditional high school choir is that Show Troupe members not only sing, but they dance. They are allowed the opportunity to sing more modern and upbeat songs, they dress in satin gowns (fitted dresses with color), and they travel during school time for performances.

Tension is strong between the two performing groups. Almost every female singer from the traditional choir auditioned, but only two were selected. The males are jealous because they feel it was not fair for Mrs. O to single out the females and exclude them from the auditions. Everyone else who was rejected, including me, wonders why we were rejected. Most of us had been performance singers in the past. We believe that if any students should have made the Show Troupe, it should at least have been those who started early.

Since our rejections, the other students and I speculate as to why Mrs. O did not choose us. Even though the high school is mostly Caucasian, some of the students believe that Mrs. O is prejudiced, which is why she only chose three black females. Another speculation is that Mrs. O wants only slim girls in Show Troupe so they will not look sloppy when they dance. I am the skinniest girl in the choir. Personally, I think Mrs. O only wants well-behaved students in the Show Troupe. Later, my speculation proves to be somewhat correct.

As if the rejection was not bad enough, what followed was even worse. Both choirs prepared for the previous concert, the annual Winter Concert. Forced to accept the rejection and move on, we continued to practice as a choir. We wholeheartedly sang our Christmas melodies and hymns out of motivation to put on a great show for our parents, teachers, and peers.

The night of the Winter Concert, the traditional choir wore black slacks, black shoes, and white, oversized, plain sweatshirts. Mrs. O should have at least gotten the name of the school printed on the shirts. Boy, we thought we were something great, maybe—after performing six songs.

However, after we exited the stage, the Show Troupe's performance took the Winter Concert from great to fantabulous.

Wearing pastel colored, satin gowns, the Show Troupe began with a melodic French song with a title I cannot even attempt to pronounce. They sang in four-part harmony, the smoothness of their voices made me envision doves soaring above the heads of the audience, peaceful and gentle. Next, clothed in gold sequined tops and black tights, they performed a jazz-like dance while singing solos. Small in stature, the soloist stood with perfect posture and a wide smile, singing both extremely high and low notes with a variety of crescendos; she was ready for Broadway. They blew the audience away with gowns in the school colors, red and black, and a three-part harmony song, "Truly," by Lionel Ritchie. With only nine girls, they sounded and looked graceful and sang even louder than us, the traditional 30-student choir. During their performance, we sat in reserved seats in the audience and watched as they received individual flowers from the teacher and what seemed like a ten-minute standing ovation from the audience. The Show Troupe showed off and stole the show.

◆ ◆ ◆

The impudent student who verbally attacks backs down and does not reply to her rhetorical question.

"I asked a question. What exactly is that supposed to mean? This is a choir. You are singers and..." I do not hear the rest of what Mrs. O says in her oft-heard motivational, instructional, suck-it-up speech. I begin doing my Japanese homework.

Two minutes later, Mrs. O jumps down my back, "Aliyana, put those papers away!"

"We are not singing right now anyway," I mumble.

"I didn't ask you what we were doing! I am trying to prepare you to become strong, professional singers." I choose not to say any of the five or six thoughts running through my head. By the end of practice, the choir is angry and disheartened.

At the conclusion of the class period, Mrs. O calls me to her piano. "Is there anything at all you feel you need to say?" she asks with a look of disgust on her face. I feel like telling her that I am good enough for the Show Troupe because I can sing and dance, and I am small in size and that until she realizes this, I will not put 100 percent effort into the traditional choir.

"I am sorry for today," I say, mentally calling myself an idiot for not saying what I really feel.

"You know, you would be an excellent addition to the Show Troupe. But it's that mouth, not paying attention, and not doing what you are told that I will not tolerate. Now, you did that last year. I do not want to go through this with you again. Do you understand?"

"Yes, ma'am," I say with a big smile, feeling privileged that she would say this to me.

"Well, you need to get your act together, young lady. OK?"

"I will."

Sadie Mae

"Hello, C.J."

"How are you, Sadie?"

"Fine. I'm just calling to tell you about those no-good people I work wit'. You know Gayle was criticizing me again today?"

"No, I didn't know that, Sadie."

"You wanna know what she said? She talkin' 'bout I come to work lookin' like I'm goin' to church. Ain't that jealousy, C.J.?"

"Yes, Sadie. I don't know how many times I have to tell you that those women are jealous of you, of how well-dressed and fine-lookin' you are."

"Yeah," I say. But I wanted to hear him say that again. "Why do they pick on me, C.J.?"

"I just told you, Sadie! You gonna let some busted and disgusted black women tear you down, then that's on you."

"Well, wha'chu' doin'?"

"I'm gettin' ready for the night service, Sadie."

"Oh, you got service tonight?" I ask, feeling my own jealousy come on. I know that C.J. likes looking at those other women. Then he acts funny toward me later when I ask questions.

"Don't start, Sadie. Yes, I have service. I gotta go, too. What are you and the kids doing today?"

"I ain't doin' nothin' wit' the kids! Wha' chu mean?"

"Ya'll not going out nowhere?"

"When do I ever feel like taking them out anywhere, C.J.?" I ask playfully, wondering what his problem is with me not taking the kids out.

"You take them out to uhh... ummm, the Golden Corral or Western Steer when I'm there."

"Yeah, that's only when you here! That's cuz you pay for it!" I say with hysterical laughter.

"Yeah, yeah, Sadie. How much did you spend today?"

Oh, shoot! I hope he did not see that shoe purchase I made yet. I bought a pair of patent leather, three-inch, gold, closed-toe shoes yesterday from the mall in Jacksonville. It should not show up on our joint bank account statement until Monday.

"Nothing really, just a few small things, that's all."

"All right, 'cause we should have at least $2,500 in the account. All right then, I'll talk to you later."

"All right, C.J. When you gonna call me back?"

"Maybe later tonight, we'll see."

"Okay, I love you."

"Love you too."

Did he just say we should have $2,500 in our account? I'm about to go buy this bad black and gold suit, to go with those shoes I just got!

Thank God I have an account with C.J.! He has really helped me out a lot. Anytime I need anything, absolutely anything, C.J. will give it up for me. I am truly blessed to have him in my life.

The Pastor

I am already sweating bullets, and I have not even said "amen" to the congregation yet. I am sitting in the speaker's seat at the host church, with the loquacious Bishop Nelson to my left and a young, anxious minister to my right who does not know if he wants to stand up or sit down.

The church itself is somewhat modern with a wide plastic chandelier over the altar area, with smaller ceiling lights surrounding it. The church has wooden pews with mauve-colored cushions. A slightly darker mauve, the freshly vacuumed carpet runs down the center aisle and across the altar. Instead of stained glass windows, this church has ordinary windows framed with flower-print valences. Sprays of flowers and brass dedication plates are easily spotted throughout the sanctuary.

The young people are already wound up... thank God, because I really do not feel like being the one to crank things up around here. Just as I predicted, I see many sets of breasts and legs, and even a couple of belly buttons and tattoos are accidentally exposed. All the while, I keep my eye on one particular girl: Kellie.

Kellie Berry is a church member's daughter who is constantly called upon to sing solos because of her angelic voice. She's a 15-year-old trapped in a 30-year-old's body. Kellie's actions say teenager, but her body says oh my, I am grown! Although lacking the shape of a Coca-Cola bottle, Kellie's body resembles a child's juice bottle—narrow at the top with a round, fat, "easy grip" bottom. Everybody, including other girls, stares at her oversized bottom, which truly makes up for her A cup breasts.

Tonight, Kellie has on black bell-bottom stretch pants that could have been painted on her body. Her clunky church heels add length to her shapely legs. Her off-black button-up blouse is not completely buttoned up, which is probably an attempt to attract attention to her barely-there breasts. Every time she raises her arms during the praise and testimony service, I catch an eyeful of belly. Kellie's face, with its Hershey-chocolate, pimple-free complexion, sports freshly plucked eyebrows that frame her almond eyes. Apparently, they were home-plucked eyebrows, with the left one sharply pointed and the other one rounded. Her shoulder length hair seems to have been dyed jet black, a superb choice against her skin. Her lips...

"Pastor Whitaker?"

"Praise Him!" I yelp, startled.

"I just asked if you would call your choir after praise and testimony, but you didn't answer. Are ya all right there?" asks Bishop Nelson.

"Yes, just thinking 'bout the goodness of Jesus!" I reply, hoping he did not catch me staring directly at Kellie.

"I thought you was meditating—my apologies for disturbing you. But we need at least two songs, even if my choir does it."

"I don't think as many of my young people showed as I hoped, but I would like to call a soloist," I reply.

"Praise God, Amen! Let God lead you, that's fine," he says, appearing satisfied with my response. I know just whose voice I want to hear.

"Praise the Lord and bless God!" I chant.

The congregation releases collective and solo "amens" simultaneously. I am glad to see they are still hyped up. Good—even if I don't really preach tonight, I can just say a lot of "God is good" statements, and they will be shouting and dancing out of the church.

"I was going to call my youth choir up, amen, but, amen, but my precious Lord, who has taken my hand and led me on to help me stand..." I suddenly forget the rest of the words after making eye contact with Kellie. All of her groupies sitting around her begin to tap her in anticipation of hearing her sing. Meanwhile, I am desperately trying to remember the rest of the song.

"I said, my precious Lord," I begin, emphasizing "precious" and "Lord" as if I am ready to preach, "who has taken my hand!" I begin to jump up and down, but remember I don't really feel like it. So I stop, but the congregation continues to jump and shout out to God. With the assistance of the organist and the drummer, six people break out in charismatic shouts.

I finish the line, "Lead me, I said leeeaaaaaaad me and help me stand!" The drummer begins to beat faster, and six more people begin to shout.

"Praise God! I would like to request for—"

Six more people begin shouting.

"Sister Kellie, would you please bless us with your rendition of..." I lose my thought when I see her begin to slowly slide lip gloss over her thin pout.

"Uhh... precious Lord! Would you please, Kellie? Any song of your choice, " I stammer.

Kellie begins to get up from her pew, signaling she will grant my request. Who would turn down the dynamic pastor who graciously goes out of town to preach, anyways?

Aliyana

I am extremely and abnormally anxious. I wake up with monster noises roaring from my stomach and feeling warm. I cannot be sick because I just got over a fever last week, or at least I hope I am not sick. The reason for my anxiety is even more unbelievable.

After finishing the Winter Concert, I cannot wait for the Spring Concert. I even have a solo in the *Phantom of the Opera* medley, "Angel of Music." Will this be a reason for my mother to come to my school? The only family members who have attended any school events I've ever been involved in have been my dad and my aunt, Melody Sue.

Aunt Melody is as sweet as candy. She's a full-time government employee and has two teenaged kids and a dog. Both her kids are active in multiple out-of-school and in-school extracurricular activities, a luxury I will never share due to my mother's constant refusal to allow me to stay after school. Both her son and daughter play for the school basketball team and take taekwondo lessons. In addition to her constant ripping and running up and down the highways behind them, Aunt Melody also takes classes for an advanced degree for a promotion on her job. Need I add that she walks the dog in the afternoons? I would think she would not have time for anything or anybody else.

My dad has really been my support through everything I've encountered. From dealing with abrasive peers to getting along with my teachers, I can bring up practically any topic with him and receive guru advice. If he ever caught wind of anyone or anything attempting to hurt his kids or his mother, he would become God-like; he would part the Red Sea for us and kill everybody else.

My dad, like my aunt, makes it a priority to attend special events that I am involved in. I make a note to myself in my journal to secretly call him when I go to my grandmother's house.

A mother is the one person that every child wants to attend special events. Otherwise, why is it that the mother has a special seat during a wedding, or is the first person to learn the date and time of a graduation? Not only is the mother wanted, but also expected—except in my household.

Once again, I knock on the judge's door, "Ma, can I come in?"

"Wha' chu' want?"

"I have to show you my clothes."

"You ain't goin' to school today cuz it's Saturday. You'll be all right. Come get this cup and bring me some ice water."

I open the door to find my mother attempting to get out of bed for the day. She is sitting straight up with the covers pushed to the side, flipping the channels on the TV.

"Nah, ya know what? I want some Mountain Dew. Bring me some Mountain Dew," she says as I stop to listen to the preacher she's watching. If I show interest in John Hagee or Rod Parsley, she might be interested in having some type of conversation with me, I think.

"What the heck you lookin' at? I told you to bring me some Mountain Dew!"

"Sorry, Ma."

I walk out of the room and into the hallway. The spotted blue carpet leads to the kitchen doorway and living room entrance. The house is not brand new, but it is fairly neat. When Dad moved his things out after the divorce, the house became much too spacious. The living room sofas, which are the same color as the spotted carpet, show the wear and tear of two working adults, two rambunctious kids, and a teenager. Behind the loveseat is a tall and dark artificial wood bookcase containing a set of blue books filled with children's Bible stories, miniature trinkets, a few spiritual self-help books, VHS movies my dad left behind, and an elephant statue made of glass marble. There was a glass living room table, but my dad broke that, as well as the TV, during the last dispute he had with my mother. Finally, the only remaining décor item in the living room, other than white lace drapes and an oversized, dusty ceiling fan, is what we call the TV stand, a table with our VCR and new TV stacked on top and VHS movies stacked neatly underneath. This stand was clearly not made to hold the TV; it is made from the same material as the bookcase, and it is beginning to split down the middle, a sign that the 17-inch is too heavy.

The starkness of the kitchen is equal to the nakedness of the living room; an oak hutch, an artificial wood dining table, and a standard refrigerator occupy most of the space. In the corner of the kitchen is a small, unoccupied area where my dad's boa constrictor cage once sat.

There have been so many occasions when my mother asks me to get her something to drink, and I want to holler, "Get it yourself!" I really do not believe the day will ever come when I will be this bold, but the thought of having that much audacity excites me anyway.

I return with the Mountain Dew and ask my mother if she wants anything else.

"Not right now, just make sure ya'll don't drink up my soda."

Finally, I release a timid, "Hey Ma, we are having our singing concert at the school soon. Can you—"

"I don't know right now, Aliyana. Now get out my room and quit bugging me! And make sure you clean up dat livin' room and kitchen."

I nervously laugh off what I decide to take as a joking comment and leave. I feel somewhat satisfied because at least she is aware now and at least she did not flat out say no (even though I have heard the answer she gave several times before, only to end in the same result: me being disappointed and her being absent).

Sadie Mae

I cannot believe C.J. has not called me yet. Where is he? What is he doing that is so important that he cannot call? Whenever this happens, I create all types of ideas and scenarios in my head while waiting for the phone to ring—car accidents, strokes, and intimacy with other women—but none of them are ever the case.

Lord, my kids are something else. Aliyana comes in here this morning looking stupid, talking about some concert. I ain't got time for no mess like that. I am working my butt off trying to keep a roof over our heads, working with a bunch of slobs who have no confidence in themselves. I know she is in the school choir; I don't have to go to the school to see that! But, every school year, it never fails: she comes into my bedroom with that stupid grin on her face harping on about an hour-long show by a bunch of kids. I think I did go to one of her programs once because I think I took Layne and Anne. But I also think I went too late and only caught the end of the performance (I didn't even see her sing). Also, Layne and Anne acted up so bad that I don't want to take them anywhere anymore.

But I'm not worried about this right now. I have to work today from 3 to 9, and I got a million things to do. I've got to drop them buzzards (my kids) off to their grandmother's house, stop by the store to see if they can order that black and gold suit in my size, and find out where C.J. is.

The Pastor

I know I have to call Sadie Mae or she is going to have a fit. Any other day she would have blown up my phone. But at least she did allow me to rest after last night.

I did not get home until after midnight. Every soul in the church wanted to say something to me after the service was over. Initially, I did not mind because I enjoy the warm and close embrace, or what I publicly call a hug, from all the ladies in the church. When they come to hug me, I pull them real close, so close that I can feel their breasts up against my body. A few times,

I have been successful with laying my hand on their bottom and kindly saying "excuse me" afterwards.

When Kellie came up for her "hug" last night, I could not wait. I gave her all kinds of accolades for her singing and encouraged her to "stay with the Lord." When she hugged me, I wrapped my arms around her waist and pulled her entire body against mine. I got an erection as soon as I felt her pelvic bone rub against me, and I think she felt it too, with her smiling self. At that moment, I made a mental note to tell her mother to make sure she gets her money in to attend the church youth trip.

I thought about that young girl all the way home. I live alone in Fayetteville, NC, at least two and a half hours from Sadie Mae, who would have been more than willing to play the role of Kellie from my fantasy, as long as she wasn't tired. Kellie would one day give such pleasure to a man that he would constantly wake up not knowing or caring what day it was. My erection remained, even when I tried to take my mind off her (temporarily) to formulate an itinerary for Sunday. I would not have been able to go to sleep with this, so I finished the job while watching clips from my "special occasion" movies.

I finally call Sadie Mae with intentions of making arrangements for a visit to her home this week.

"Hello, Sadie."

"Hey C.J. I thought you said you were gonna call last night?"

"No, I told you maybe later and I would see."

"Oh. How was the service? "

"Blessed."

"That's it? What did you preach about?"

"I just encouraged the youth to follow God, that's all."

"Oh... Wha' chu doin'?"

"Just got up, thinking about whether or not I'm gonna come up there this week—"

"You comin' up here? When?" Sadie sounds extremely elated. This will be a great opportunity. "I'm comin' to see you, Sadie."

"Oh, you are! You can come on up here. I'll be here. I gotta work Monday night and maybe Tuesday, though."

"That's all right. I'll watch the kids for you."

"Oh, all right. Wha' chu wanna eat when you come up here? Are you comin' Sunday or Monday?"

"I will probably leave right after church and just have my stuff in the trunk... be there by Sunday night, stay 'til Wednesday."

Aliyana

After cleaning the kitchen, living room, my half of the bedroom, and the bathroom, I am tired as crap. My mother is constantly barking, "Clean up my house!" but she just sits in her bed and watches TV and calls us to run her errands. If it is her house, why can't she clean it herself sometimes or at least help?

Because I am the oldest, I end up doing most of the housecleaning. I do understand that every child needs to be trained, but that is exactly my point. I wasn't trained or shown what to do. I was told to do things and then got slapped if it was done wrong.

"Aliyana, wha' chu doin'?" My mother hollers from her bed.

"I just washed the dishes and swept the floor."

"Did you clean off da table and clean dat microwave out?"

"Yeah."

"Yeah?" she asks rhetorically, challenging my grammar.

"Yes." I feel like asking her to bring me a soda. "I am getting ready to vacuum the floor in the livin' room."

"Hurry up so you can clean out dat bathroom. It's filthy! And make sure you clean out that tub too!"

I turn on the vacuum cleaner and begin to sob. I do not know how many times I have cried while having the vacuum cleaner going, but it has been quite often and is somewhat effective. I sometimes envision myself as a modern Cinderella. I am made to do all the cleaning in the house, while my mother sits in her bed drinking sodas, Layne pretends to clean her half of the bedroom, and Anne is too young to help so she just follows me around (hey, at least I got some type of support). I finish the living room.

One of my pet peeves is to clean an area or a room and as soon as I finish, someone else rushes to the area as if it was cleaned just for them. I feel I have the right to enjoy the clean area first if I cleaned it. Besides, I am not the only one living in this house, but it sure seems like I am the only one cleaning it. As soon as I finish cleaning and step out of the bathroom, here comes my mother with her clothes, ready to funk it up again. She should have at least cleaned the bathroom if she was planning on using it first.

I go to clean my bedroom finally. However, to me, it is already clean.

The bedroom has two tall oak dressers, which sit side by side against one wall. Beside them is a closet made for a single person, but shared by Layne and me. Against opposite walls are two twin beds, both adorned with matching Sesame Street comforters.

One good thing about not being able to have friends over is at least they won't see my embarrassing, childish bedroom! A high school student with elementary bed sheets... what happened to the flowers, stars, and peace signs?

When my mother tells me to clean up the bedroom, she means the entire room. But I do not create a mess in the entire room. After all of my cleaning "training," I find that I am a serious neat freak. As soon as I wake, I make up my bed. My shoes are lined up in two categories, dress shoes and sneakers, under my bed. I have a CD player sitting on top of my dresser, and each individual dresser drawer houses my neatly stacked, oversized, hand-me-down clothes from my mother. The only other area I occupy in this room is my half of the closet, which contains a few hanging winter coats and small personal items neatly stacked on the shelf. In the end, when all of the areas I just mentioned are neat, I feel that this means I cleaned the room.

Then there is Layne, my wonderfully messy 10-year-old sister. I consider her space wonderfully messy because I frequently wonder how she can stand to sleep, eat, and reside in her area. As soon as she wakes, she leaves her tossed and mangled bed for the bathroom. I figure she cleans herself up because she pees in the bed every single night. Layne pees in the bed so much that there is an imprint of her butt in the middle of the bed with heavy and dark yellow, orange, and brown stains. Who should be made to clean up the bedroom? Her shoes are nowhere in sight under her bed because everything she owns is thrown underneath it: clothes, books, shoes, food, silverware, Barbie dolls, papers, and various other items. She cannot find her textbooks at the end of the school year, but often finds them after the fact somewhere under that bed. If I am not careful, some of my things could end up inside her never-ending whirlpool of junk. The same concept applies to the top and insides of her dresser, which is closest to the door and continuously within eyesight of my mother, and her half of the closet. In the end, when all of the areas Layne occupies are messy, my mother feels that this means I did not clean the room.

I begin using pine cleaner (which is pointless because the smell of pine in combination with the other strong liquid soaking Layne's bed smells worse) to clean off my CD player and dresser.

"What the hell did I tell ya to do, Aliyana!" my mother yells as I jump two feet back, startled because I didn't see her come out of the bathroom.

"You keep right on defying me, and I am going to tear you up!"

How did I defy her when I already cleaned three rooms of the house?

"I am cleaning the room, " I timidly say.

"Who do you think you are talking to? I told ya to clean this room! There is still crap all over the dresser, under the bed!"

"I just cleaned my dresser off."

Mommy obviously does not like my answer or cleaning skills because she walks up to me and slaps me across my face. The sting makes me feel like I received a paper cut across my cheek. I begin to sob, not from the direct blow, but because my mother stands in front of me for what seems like five minutes (it was probably only 40 seconds or so) with a look of disgust on her face. She looks at me with a smirk, and the look of hate is so strong in her eyes that I suddenly do not feel like her daughter, but a beast from the woods that just invaded her home. Is she a slave master reincarnate?

"Clean this room up! That is your sister, I don't care whose side of the room it is," she says as she walks into her bedroom.

I slowly walk over to Layne's bed and begin pulling clothing items from underneath it, one by one, folding them, then laying them in a pile on her bed. Mommy then calls Layne to help me. She was in the living room (after I just cleaned it up) playing with Anne and the Barbie dolls she could find from her mess.

Sadie Mae

As I dry off after my shower, I anxiously wait for C.J. to get here. He is the only man who has ever treated me like I am worth anything. He gives me money, not only for bills, but for personal spending too. He bought me a car (and put it on his insurance), and he... well, men do not know how treat women, and I know this from my experience with Richard Taylor, who is a menace to society and my life.

We dated around for a while during my high school days. He was so handsome then: tall, light-skinned, well built but slim, and had a charming smile. What made him even more attractive was the fact that he would tell me how pretty I was. We met when I was 16. I was always shy and timid around boys, but I did not believe that I was naïve. At 16, I was just as stunning as he was. Wearing a size 4, I was slim with what I called a big old booty! I was mostly noticed for my fair skin and thick, long hair. I have almond-shaped eyes because of my family's Native American lineage. I also have strong facial features: high cheek bones and fingernail-deep dimples.

I do not remember how we met (I have forcibly made myself forget all things that pertain to him), but I do remember him telling me about how he was planning on going into the Marine Corps and taking classes to become a disc jockey. I just knew he would have enough money to support me and my potential spending habits, so I readily accepted his offers to go out occasionally. Little did I know that one of those occasions would cost me eight years of my life.

Within months, I realized that I was pregnant. At the age of 17, unmarried and not yet a high school graduate, I gave birth to a baby girl. Aliyana, named by her daddy, unknowingly had become the first of many horrid events in my life.

The smell of mushy peas, roast beef, and dead roses filled the sitting room of the busy hospital. In all corners of the room there was crying. In the center of the room, vivid emotions blaring anger and hurt caused my newborn, Aliyana, to cry.

"You are going to bust hell wide open with yo' fat mouth! You always sticking your nose in everybody else's business! You a good-for-nothin' old hag! Shut up, just shut up!" Richard shouted in my mother's face.

"I'll kill you, bastard! You don't mess with my daughter! Call the Sheriff if ya wan' ter, I *am* the Sheriff!" my mother shouted back at him so hard that half of her words were incomprehensible.

In an instant, Richard drew back his right arm and socked my mother in her left eye. Ever since that day, the day of Aliyana's birth, I have felt sorrow and shame for dating and marrying that man. He destroyed my childhood—well, I guess I cannot totally blame this on him since I was willing to create Aliyana. But he definitely destroyed me mentally and later attempted to do so physically.

Aliyana

I am still working on Layne's side of the room after an hour. I am not even halfway done pulling the junk from under her bed, and she is not helping me. She will find something that she has missed for a while and then get off track. She just found her princess Barbie, missing the princess gown and one shoe, and now she is sitting on the side of the bed combing the doll's hair.

As much I cannot stand my mother right now, I used to feel sorry for her.

❖ ❖ ❖

After kneeling beside my bed to say my prayers for the second time, I could hear my parents in the living room fighting over the bills. The quarrel would end soon because my father was a police officer, and he usually worked late at night. I felt really sorry for my mother because he constantly fought with her. I just knew she had to feel sorry for us, too, because my father also hit us with his leather police belt. I hoped at that moment that he would not hit her with it.

I reached for my glasses so I could read the time on the clock. At 2:34 in the morning, my mother was crying hard and loud as my father yelled with no end in sight.

"Get up off the darn floor before I hit you again!"

"Please don't hit me... stop... I can't..."

I heard a sharp striking noise and a dish breaking. It sounded like human flesh in contact with leather.

"Get out if you don't want to pay the darn bills!"

I heard my father walking down the hall, so I quickly closed my eyes just in case he walked into our room. While my eyes were closed, I pictured my father standing over my mom in the kitchen, hitting her with his leather police belt.

My mom was sobbing in the kitchen. I wished I could go and pick her up off the floor and tell her that everything would be fine, but I was just as scared as she was. I was not scared of my father, who would take me out for vanilla cones dipped in chocolate and bite the tip off just to make me laugh, and who would smile at me and ruffle my already ruffled hair... But I was afraid of the vein in his forehead that pulsed with rage, the bloody fist that busted through the glass in the front door, and the hand that held the hammer when it shattered the television screen. Mommy believed in God though. I was sure that God would let her know that everything would be fine.

Someone walked in the room, quietly and slowly, but I did not know who it was. I heard the rattling of a bag and my closet door opening.

Mommy whispered, "Aliyana, get up! Get up and put your clothes on."

"Okay Ma, are you going to be all right?" I said as I jumped out of the bed and threw on a pair of jeans. Still sobbing, she did not answer me. She was taking some of our clothes out of the closet and packing them in large, black garbage bags that she had sneaked out of the kitchen under her robe.

"Where are we going this early in the morning?" I thought about grabbing my book bag, since I had to go to school the next day. Again, I received no response from my mother.

Mommy awakened Layne and removed Anne, who was only a few months old, from the crib wrapped in the blanket she had been sleeping in. She was struggling to keep her purse on her shoulder and carry the baby at the same time. I started to take it from her, and I noticed a deep wound and blood on her arm. I knew my dad had hurt her.

"Ma, let me take the purse off your shoulder so you can put your coat on." I could tell she was appreciative when she sighed, but she did not speak a word as I carefully guided the purse off her arm. Mommy's injury looked like a vicious animal had attacked her. *Maybe one did*, I thought, angry at my dad.

Mommy, my two sisters, and I left the house, dressed for winter, without my father. We walked to the nearest pay phone.

❖ ❖ ❖

Mommy will not mistreat us, I tell myself now, folding more clothes that do not belong to me.

Sadie Mae

I hate Richard for what he did to me. He is as good as a million-dollar check written a decade ago. And his kids look and act just like him. That is why I am sick of them!

"Aight ya'll! Time to cut the grass! Put some old clothes on and come on outside!" I yell.

The Pastor

A man of God has to be sharp when he steps up in the place. He has to be so sharp that the members who walk past him on either side get cut. Sharp enough to stab onlookers in their drooling eyes. Sharp enough to sting the celibate woman who said she did not want a man.

For the Sunday services tomorrow, I am looking for that sharp "Pow!" and "Ouch!" outfit in my closet. Just like my mother and Sadie Mae, I like to dress well and look distinguished. With over 25 different suits in my closet, I have enough to choose from (that is enough for a different suit every Sunday for six months). The church took up collections and offerings and bought some of my suits for special events: Pastor Anniversary, my birthday, Christmas, etc. My secretary, Sidney, has my Italian suit measurements down pat (with her fine self, I could make her the first lady of the church, with her long hair, light skin, and natural green eyes). Just in case she ever forgets, she knows the measurements can be found in my office desk, bottom drawer, left side, written on an index card.

Towards the middle of the freshly tailored suits, all hanging in order from light-colored to dark-colored, I spot my choice: a navy blue with pink pinstripes, Italian Kenneth Cole original. I think about going all out and wearing a pink-collared shirt with matching pink patent leather/alligator skin shoes, but seeing all of the pink brings to mind unpleasant memories of my youth.

❖ ❖ ❖

It was the beginning of middle school for me. I was in seventh grade, and after being in school only two weeks, I had just passed my science test, which I had been afraid I would fail. When the bell rang, I rushed to my locker, anxious to put away the test to show my mother later. As soon as I stepped into the hall, a group of four black eighth-grade boys approached me.

"Ooooh! Look how sweet our little C.J. looks today!" one of the boys said. The other three boys burst out in hysterical laughter. Being a lower-classman at school, I was too afraid to defend myself. So the taunting continued.

"Yeah! He look like the new kind of M&Ms. He melts in yo' mouth *and* in yo' hand!" another boy chimed in as he made private male sexual gestures in my face.

"Where yo' mamma get that cute little pink shirt that you tucked so neatly in yo' little shorts?" The boys were laughing so hard they now had an audience encircling us. All I could do was stand there. *Why don't you just run, you idiot? I couldn't figure out what to do. Punch him in his big, liver-lip mouth and he will shut-up.*

As I was contemplating my next move, one of the boys shoved me into the audience. I fell to the floor, dropping all of my books and my science test.

"Oh, look Gary! Little Ms. C.J. passed his test!"

"That is because all he do is sit in his room at night and study and dress like a girl!"

"You don't even know me, man! Why you actin' like this?" I finally said. I heard someone from the audience say, "It's about time he said something for himself!"

One of the four boys pushed my head again so hard that I fell backward, still lying in the middle of the floor. I felt an intense throbbing along the side of my forehead—that little sucker must have cut me with his fingernail!

"Hey! You cut me with yo' nail, ya jerk!" I screamed.

"Aww, you just mad cause yo' nails ain't as long as mine! You want to paint my nails, don't ya, C.J.?"

"Yeah, he wanna paint 'em pink," called a member of the audience.

Just as one of the boys was going to push or hit me again, my science teacher, a short and slinky white man with a bow tie, walked out into the hall.

"All right people, move it! Move it! Class starts in two minutes, let's go!"

As the crowd dissipated, many of the kids, who were mostly black, walked away calling me "gay," "pinky," and "Barbie dog." From that day forward, I was known as the homosexual who wore pink to school.

Aliyana

Mommy is using her John Deere knock-off to cut her two acres of grass. While she sits and rides around, with a wide-brim, straw summer hat and a bottle of water in the hand she is not using to navigate the lawn mower, she instructs Layne to rake up the grass behind her. My job is to collect the grass by picking up clumps of it in my hand and toss it in large garbage bags. After only five minutes, my hands are turning red and ferociously itchy. I try to pick up more grass and at least finish the pile I started. The more grass I touch, the more my hands itch. Scratching my hands apparently is not the cure.

"Ma! Ma!" I try to yell over the lawn mower, waving my arms so that my mother will see me. But she rides right on past.

"Ma!" I scream as she finally comes to a stop.

"Wha' chu want?" she asks with irritation.

"I think I am allergic to this cut grass!" What do I know? I really only assume that I am allergic because my hands itch. I have heard other people say they get rashes and itching from being allergic to certain foods.

"What in the crap you talkin' 'bout?"

"I think I'm allergic to the grass. See..." I show her my hands, which are now red over the entire palms and my wrists.

"Aliyana, go on out there and pick up dat grass and stop playing in it! And hurry up!" she screams over the motor of the lawn mower.

Playing in it? Who was playing in the grass?

I begin crying. How in the world am I supposed to finish picking up the grass with all of this unbelievable itching going on? At this point, I am extremely angry at my mother. I feel that she does not care about me, so why should I care about me? This thought gives me a new determination: I will pick up all of the grass and hope that my hands swell so bad that I cannot do anything else today. Anne finds me bent over the grass with large tears falling from my cheeks onto the ground and runs over to help me. "You wan' me to help ya, Aliyana?" she asks.

I do not reply, which I guess is very insolent of me. But I just do not care anymore about anything. I begin crying harder and louder. First, because my hands are now stinging and itching at the same time. Second, because I do not know what I would do without my sweet, *sweet* sister, Anne.

By the time I reach my last two piles of cut grass, both my mother and Layne are finished, both sitting on the porch drinking water, watching Anne and me.

❖ ❖ ❖

Mommy drops all of us off at Grandma Ann's house. Grandma Ann has triple the amount of yard that my mother has, and she uses it resourcefully. Grandma Ann has an old, rusty, tin roof and cinder block barn, an old wooden shed that looks as if it would fall if whispered to, a grape vineyard with two clotheslines directly across from it, a homemade hog pen, a chicken house, apple and plum trees, and two driveways, and there is still plenty of yard space. I often go out into the backyard and exercise or run around, listening to my Walkman. However, when I start, it is hard for me to stop.

"Aliyana!" Anne runs up to me with a look of urgency. "Grandma Ann has been calling you for a while, but you won't come in!"

"Oh, I didn't hear her."

I go into Grandma Ann's house after two and a half hours of "exercising." The inside of the house is dark, especially compared to the light of the warm sun I am protected by while in the backyard. The walls are dark brown artificial wood. The couches are black, and the doors are dark mahogany. The floor-model color television is being closely studied by Layne, who has probably been sitting in front of it since we arrived. My mute grandpa is sitting on the same couch and in the same spot that he sits in every single day. He is only "mute" because he does not want to be attacked by Grandma Ann, who will cuss him out for simple things, like not making her ice water the way she wants it or for disclosing that he is hungry.

Grandma Ann's house has absolutely no air conditioning. Fans are supposed to condition a person to feel artificial air, but even the fans seem to be blowing around heat waves. As a result, everyone is sweating. The damp moisture from the old house combined with heat and no circulating air equals a stench of old food and a boys' locker room after a football game. Everything in the house smells aged.

"Dang," I say when I walk into the house. It smells so bad that I almost do not want to touch anything, fearing that items around me will contaminate me. I do faintly smell what seems to be pork chops and onions in gravy, one of Grandma Ann's specialties.

"C'm'ere, Aliyana, I wan' cha to read dis to me," Grandma Ann says as she motions for me to sit beside her, on *her* couch. Normally, we do not have permission to sit on her couch. Behind it is all of her mail, bills, and letters, and her Butterfinger candy bars, which we can only have a piece of once she opens one. She claims that she needs them because she is diabetic; however, I am the current chosen one because she wants me to read her horoscope to her.

❖ ❖ ❖

I miss my dad. In my eyes, he is a celebrity. Whenever I get the chance to see him, I am filled with butterflies, joy, and a slight trace of drool in anticipation of his hug, gentle kiss on my cheek, and sweet scent of cologne. However, these special occasions do not occur frequently. As a result, I have to find other means of contacting him.

In the past, I tried writing my dad by mail. These long, colorful pieces of writing were easy to create but hard to ship off. I was constantly discouraged after asking my whole family for just a single stamp and not receiving a single one. Finally, I had to ask my mother, who questioned me as if I were asking for access to a nuclear bomb: *Wha' 'chu need it for? Where are you sending a letter to? Why? Who told you to write a letter in my house?* I would tell her that I was sending a letter to my friend Amy from school. She would reluctantly give me a stamp, yelling that I need to talk to Amy at school and stop writing "all those crazy letters because they ain't sayin' nothin' noways." The thing is, my mother is nosy and does not trust me. She would go to the mailbox after I put the letter in the box with the flag up on my way to school and check to see what I was actually mailing. She would take the letter out, read it, beat me when I returned from school, and then keep the letter and read it to five or six people she would call that night. I only attempted to contact him twice this way, and both attempts were unsuccessful.

Since my dad left the police department a year ago for reasons that I am still unsure of, he developed a passion for being a disc jockey and worked at a local radio station. When mailing him letters didn't work, I tried a different form of contact. He frequently visits car dealerships in an attempt to promote his radio show. I know where a few of these dealerships are located, so when I knew where he was promoting, I tried to endear myself to either Grandma Ann or Grandpa. I would clean their house a little harder, eat a little more food (Grandma Ann loves when someone asks for seconds or thirds of her country cooking), and be a lot nicer and talk sweet to them. By the close of two hours of doing all of these things, I would have them ready to go for a ride, where we would just happen to stop at the dealership.

I really don't know what I was thinking. Grandma Ann absolutely detests my dad. Once, after she figured out what I did, she was cordial with my dad when she saw him, but she was steaming and couldn't wait to get back home to tell my mom who she saw.

Not only would she tell my mother who she saw, but Grandma Ann would also tell her he gave me money, which my mother took from me, claiming that she needed it "because he doesn't pay his child support." Grandma Ann would even add fictitious people to the story that would cause my mother to become angry enough to tear my butt up.

"Yeah, he had some woman out there, hugged up all on him...," Grandma Ann lied.

"He did what?" my mother asked with a combination of shock and anger.

"Yeah, he had another baby out there too."

"No, Grandma, no he didn't," I proclaimed.

"You shut up. Just shut up. Ain't nobody tell you to go out there no way. Why did you take her out there, Ma?" my mother asked.

"Aliyana told me she wanted to go for a ride."

Well, there it was. The switch, a branch from a tree. The floor. The ceiling. The smack across my face because apparently the switch broke. The blood coming from my legs. My sobbing. My excitement of seeing Dad diminished by the pain of my beating.

Oh well, at least I got to see my dad.

The second "ride" was much more successful. Grandpa, real laid back, likes my dad. I could tell because he would frequently ask me questions about him and his work. Although I truly did not know sometimes, I boldly stated to Grandpa that my dad was fine and that he asked about him too. This always made Grandpa smile. I feel that I did not lie to Grandpa because my dad did ask about him, but only when I was able to talk to him. So the few times I asked Grandpa to go for a "ride," he agreed and was just as excited as I was to get out of the house. Afterwards, when my mother came to pick my sisters and me up, Grandpa did not say a word.

Currently, I am trying to contact my dad by calling him from Grandma Ann's house. Grandma Ann is prone to listen in on the calls, then tell my mother everything she hears, plus extra. So I wait for her to leave the house. She announces that she is going to visit her girlfriends and drink a little liquor, also known as Pepsi (Grandma Ann claims she gets drunk from

Pepsi. If she asks me, it is only a sugar rush for an old, diabetic woman).

Grandma Ann prepares to leave by putting on two bras, two dresses, a sweater, and a coat. Need I remind her that it is 88 degrees outside? I do not really care, as long as she leaves. My only goal at this one moment is reaching my dad.

Grandma Ann finally leaves, taking my whining and begging sister, Layne.

"Can I go, huh? Grandma, can I go?"

"Go where?"

"Wit' chu?"

"You don't even know where I'm goin'. C'mon, child."

Layne packs up all of her Barbie dolls, grinning from ear to ear as if she has won a pageant.

As soon as I see her 1994 white Ford Escort drive out of sight, I rush to the phone, dialing my dad's number almost with my eyes closed.

"KISS FM!"

"Hey Dad," I exclaim at the sound of his voice.

"Hey there, darling! What are you up to?"

"Nothing. I'm at Grandma's house, and she just left, so I wanted to call you real quick."

"Oh, yeah? Glad to hear it. It's always good to hear from my lovely daughter," he says.

"When are we going to be able to see you again?"

My dad clears his throat. "I'm not sure. What's your mom talking about? I mean, as far as visitation on the weekends and all."

"It's not looking good, Dad. She said that ever since that time you refused to let Pastor Whitaker's mom pick us up from the magistrate, she probably won't take us back. Why do we have to meet at the courthouse just to get picked up anyways?"

"Well, you know, Aliyana, that's just the way it is sometimes, when two people don't get along."

"Aunt Melody doesn't drop her kids off at no courthouse," I reply, angry.

"I know. It's ridiculous. But, I'll settle for whatever I can get to see my kids. Ya know what I mean?"

"Yeah," I reply, feeling hopeless.

"Hey, cheer up. It's all right, Aliyana. Keep ya head up," my dad says.

"I miss you, Dad. I wish I could live with you."

"Well, that seems to be a battle I can't win. If I ask the court for custody, they are going to look at my trailer compared to the house, which I did pay for, by the way. The court system is really unfair. If they looked at how I was treated by your mother and other key factors, maybe they would reconsider. But, I really think the court system favors women. Everywhere I look, the mothers have custody of the children. Anyways, Aliyana, I don't want to bore you."

"You are fine, Dad," I say, thinking to myself that my dad could never bore me. Everything he ever says is a sweet melody of angelic music that I never want to stop playing.

Sadie Mae

I can't wait for C.J. to arrive. I went shopping for groceries, spending more than I should, in order to have the best in the house for his arrival: shrimp, steaks, salad mixes, and all kinds of breakfast foods. I also bought food—chicken, cereal, and milk—for the kids. I feel that the kids are too young (and expensive since I have three) to appreciate fine foods.

Lately, I am finding myself yelling too much at the kids, but only because they act like they can't hear. I had to tell Aliyana four times to clean the kitchen, and then she goes and washes the dishes only and then claims to be done. I had to tell her to sweep and mop the floor, clean the table, and clean the inside and outside of the refrigerator and microwave. Also, if I hear that child of mine mumbling under her breath again when I ask her to do something, I am going to beat her with a switch from outside while she is naked. I wasn't raised to be disrespectful, and I'll be damned if I raise a disrespectful child, especially when she lives in the house and eats the food that I pay for. Ungrateful, that's what I call it.

I made Anne sweep off the porch and Layne vacuum the living room floor. While Anne performed her task with haste, I had to actually show Layne how to vacuum because she would claim to be done while I could still see cotton ball pieces staring back at me. Layne acted like she was scared to push the vacuum cleaner around the corners of the sofas and tables, or maybe she was just being lazy and did not want to do it at all.

Overall, I got the house ready for C.J.'s arrival. After cutting the grass this morning and cleaning the house tonight, I am exhausted. I begin to read my Bible, knowing that I probably will not make it past two verses since I get so sleepy while reading. However, I need to brush up on my spiritual knowledge so that I can show C.J. how much I know.

Aliyana

I wake to the sound of my mother's dog-like wake-up call, a barking that never ends until it receives complete and total satisfaction from a human.

"Aliyana, get up! It's time to get up!"

"Okay, Ma."

"Wha' chu say? It's 5 o'clock."

"I heard you, Ma," I reply, rolling out of the bed to follow my regular morning routines.

Every morning after I finish my birdbath or, when I am allowed to take one, short shower, I turn the water off and listen for my mom's complaint. Usually, right after I wash up, my mom will begin to criticize how much water I use. To my surprise, I hear nothing. After contemplating whether to attempt to turn the shower back on for a few more minutes, I assume she is simply sleeping hard.

My mom hates when we wear anything close to fitted, but I thought that I would try to wear a T-shirt one of my friends gave me for my birthday. It was clearly a cheap shirt, but cute for school; it was a white cotton T-shirt with a screen-print design of a kitten with a compassionate look on her face. I would normally wear this shirt underneath something my mom bought, but I wanted her to finally see it so I could get the "where did you get that from?" over with. I quickly brush over my braided hair and go to knock on my mom's door.

The first knock is light, and I get no response. I figure she did not hear me, so I knock again, slightly harder. After still not hearing a response, I call out to her, "Ma?"

"Wha' chu want? Stop knocking on the door," she replies. She sounds as if she is purposely speaking low, but why?

"Don't you have to see my clothes?"

"No, you know wha' chu supposed to wear to school."

I cannot believe what I am hearing. My interrogating, army-sergeant mother has never allowed me, the helpless cadet, to go to school without the morning checkup.

I almost leap into my room with excitement that I do not have to go on trial this morning and happy that I can now take my braids out and wear my hair the way I choose, since my mother will not see it anyway. I will have to remember to put the hideous, loose cornrows back in before she arrives home from work tonight.

Oh Lord, I thank you for this day! I pray in a whisper as I open the front door, just as I discover the reason for the good fortune of my mother not opening her door. Beside her Lincoln Continental is a shiny, clean, winter white Cadillac.

Pastor Whitaker is visiting.

❖ ❖ ❖

I am sitting in Mrs. O's class, not paying attention since she is teaching the tenors their part, trying to convince myself that I am not angry. I mean, why should I be? If my mother wants to date, hang with, or even sleep with Mr. Whitaker, why should it bother me?

I reach up to touch my hair while trying my best not to attract attention to myself. The last time I attempted to pull a stunt with my hair like the one I am pulling today, I learned a valuable lesson about African American hair: a girl's hair can be long when wet, but when it dries up, it shrinks and shortens. Once, I wet my hair in the girls' bathroom to find it hanging down my back and wetting the back of my shirt. I did not care if my shirt was wet, as long as I could swing and show off my hair. Well, I only wet it once that day, and by my last-period class, my hair resembled cotton balls, dyed black and refusing to absorb any moisture. Even though a friend braided it for me on the bus ride home that afternoon, my mother still knew that I had wet my hair because of the puffiness of the ends and the crookedness of the new braids.

Today, I keep wetting my hair to ensure that it is still long in length and flowing. Of course the back of my shirt has been wet all day, but it was hardly noticeable after I put back on my cheap, black T-shirt that has a silver Japanese symbol for love on the front after school administrators told me the kitten shirt was not allowed because of the spaghetti straps.

But of course, there is always that group of retards who is looking too hard at me, who locates that weakness that I have tried to hide.

I notice them snickering and on the verge of saying something aloud that will make me feel like a groundhog that is not ready for February 2, not wanting to ever come out of hiding. Before they have the opportunity to demean me, I try to leave the class.

"Mrs. O, can I go to—"

"Excuse me? Young lady, excuse me!" she yells. I can feel myself melting inside for making the situation worse. Now, everyone in the class has their eyes resting on me, and possibly my hair too.

"Sorry, Mrs. O."

"Sorry doesn't cut it, young lady. You sit over there and daydream, then yell out in the middle of class?" Mrs. O makes a terribly angry face at me, one eyebrow reaching for the other in confusion, a smirk on sharper than Elvis' grin. Without looking, I can detect that the group I was trying to avoid are struggling to hold in their laughter. At this moment, I wish someone somewhere would pull the fire alarm.

"Now that you have taken all of my attention from the class, what do you want, Aliyana?" Mrs. O asks as she leans on the piano with her arms crossed as if at war.

"I just wanted to know if I could go to the bathroom," I mumble.

"What?" she says, holding her hand to her ear. "I cannot hear you if you are talking to yourself!"

One of the dark-skinned girls from the group blurts out, "She said can she go to the bathroom to put some water in that nappy head so she can try to look like a white girl!" The entire class, with the exception of my friends in the soprano section, erupts in laughter. When Mrs. O begins her attempt to show her disapproval of the comment that the burnt piece of meat just made, I run out of the room in tears, swinging my hair behind me.

Pastor Whitaker

When I walk in the house, the scents of fresh lemons and new wood furniture seem to not only fill my nostrils but also my pores. Although there is no new furniture to be found, each piece of furniture within my sight is as clean as fresh snow, with no dust in sight. I actually look inside the glass living room table to make sure I still look handsome. The house was well prepared for my visit, and I feel welcome. At home.

Sadie Mae, trying her best not to reveal excitement and anxiety in her voice about my visit, calls half an hour after arriving at work and asks me to see to it that her kids arrive home safely from school, eat dinner, and go to bed by nine. With only a teenager and two kids that are still enamored with Barbie, I feel this will be an extremely easy task.

Of course I do not feel like cooking after my long drive from Fayetteville to New Bern, so I plan to wait until the girls get home from school and take them to Burger King.

I set down my bags in the feminine bedroom, Sadie Mae's haven and previous hell. In this room, she was romanced and beaten by her then husband. Sometimes when I look around the room, I feel like I can still see the dark red blood splotches on the wall from when he broke into the house by punching his fist through a glass window in the door and went on a rampage destroying the family furnishings throughout the house. He claimed he wanted to beat me, but I ran. Why? I am too pretty to get dirty. I will fight a man if I have to, but I didn't have to.

❖ ❖ ❖

That night was a tumultuous one. If only I had stayed away until the next morning as planned. But

Sadie Mae wanted me to come over. Yes, her divorce was not finalized, but what is done is done: they were separated. Two puzzle pieces separated and stretched, not to ever fit each other again. That stretch was blamed on me.

Richard knocked on the door while we were sitting in the living room. Sadie Mae claimed to have just gotten out of bed, wearing an oversized, grandma-like nightshirt, but she had no clothes on underneath. Cool from the ceiling fan, Sadie Mae's nipples had hardened and attempted to seek the outside world, jailed by the cotton fabric. Naturally, this turned me on.

What turned me off were the knocks at the door. After two knocks, there was a series of bangs. I knew that if her husband got into the house, there would be pain: the pain he would feel from witnessing me sitting in his living room with his half-dressed wife; the pain she would feel from the guilt of sitting there with me; the pain we could both feel of violence.

After finding a spot to keep my suitcase for my two-day visit, I admire the few pictures of Sadie Mae on the wall. It seems odd to me that she would have pictures of herself on the headboard of her own bed, but then again I have pictures of myself throughout my house. I have always thought Sadie to be one of the most beautiful Redbones I have ever seen. Even in our youth, when our mothers would get together, I thought Sadie Mae was one of the prettiest girls in the world.

I hear a clicking noise outside the bedroom and peep out to check on it. It sounds as if a key is turning the lock. Layne opens the door with such force that I assume she will fall. She unlocked the door with a key attached to a dirty shoestring hanging from her neck. She is still bent over the knob after lazily unlocking the door without taking the key off her neck. She yelps when she sees me approach her.

Layne is a chubby but tall girl. She always looks at me as if she had just seen a spider crawling up her sleeve. With her long and untamed hair falling around her face, I sometimes catch a whiff of girl who is not yet taught to use deodorant. Layne bothers me because I feel like she sees more into me than I want her to.

"Go take those books and book bags straight to your room. Don't just put them down in the living room," I say to her in my "don't bother me" voice.

Anne follows closely behind Layne, grinning and struggling to keep her books from falling out of her torn book bag.

Anne is a sweet girl who is always smiling through missing teeth, always attempting to keep her clothes neat while her dark and never-met-a-perm hair remains matted, dry, and dull, always speaking to me when she sees me, as if I am her father.

I ask Anne, "What time does Aliyana usually get home from school?"

"I don't know what time, but after us," she replies through two missing teeth and an innocent smile.

Ready to relax for the evening, I decide to pick Aliyana up from school.

I stroll to my 1996 off-white, leather-top Cadillac. The four-door model was such a smooth sight and a black man's joy. The interior, light ivory-colored leather seats, always seem to envelop my body in cushion and comfort, unimaginable with just any old car.

I start the quiet engine while Anne and Layne, knowing how angry I get about jumping around my car, carefully climb inside. Judging by the anxious and anticipatory looks on their faces, it seems as if they anticipate my scrutiny. Anne's door is not even closed entirely because she is so afraid of slamming it.

"I got it," I yelp as I get out of the car to close the door properly. Anne sits still, quiet and motionless.

Our ride to New Bern High School is a very quiet one. The kids simply stare out of the window, the engine purrs, and I sporadically hum. Growing weary of the quiet, I turn on the jazz music radio station just as I notice that Layne raises her hand, seemingly to touch the window of the car.

"Don't put your fingerprints on my window. Keep your hands down," I say with so much authority that she seems to be startled. Layne makes a face of disgust and crosses her arms.

As I slowly pull up to the school, half fearing that one of the impudent teens will damage my Cadillac in some way, I squint in an attempt to locate Aliyana. There are so many young men and women standing outside. Some are dressed in gothic clothing, all black, with spiky hair and dangling chains. Some are dressed as athletes ready for some type of sports practice.

Sitting around the benches is a group dressed in what the youth call "prep" clothes, fitted jeans and tops with a pair of heels and V-neck, pastel-colored sweaters tied around their waists. There are a couple of black kids wearing oversized starter jackets and bulky tennis shoes. They are the loudest group, cursing and singing. Finally, there is a group of students, not dressed in any particular way, not belonging to any clique, just standing around and watching the other groups. They are a mixture of black, white, Asian, and Filipino kids. From this group, Aliyana emerges.

She strolls toward the car wearing a plain hunter green T-shirt and baggy white jeans that seem to make her hips look like a size 5 or 6, which seems odd attached to her pencil-thin arms and narrow waist. It almost looks as if she stuffed her pants with fabric. She plops down on the seat of the car and carefully closes the door. Both Layne and Anne chime in at the same time, "Hey Aliyana."

"Hey," Aliyana replies with a tone of depression as she stares straight ahead out of the front window.

"What is wrong?" I ask.

"I'm fine."

When she replies this way, I know that means something similar to "not right now" or "I don't want to talk about it." I let the conversation go as I contemplate how I will return to it later.

"Whatever happened today, don't let it get you down. You are too beautiful of a young lady to let any of these little kids get to you. You hear me?"

"Yes, sir," she replies, finally allowing a smile to appear on her honey-colored face of flawless skin.

❖ ❖ ❖

While watching the kids eat, I notice that Aliyana does not make eye contact with me or her sisters, she doesn't say one word, and she doesn't crack a smile. I figure she is either upset at her mother, who constantly chastises her for the smallest thing, or something happened at school. I didn't think that her last conversation with her mother went badly. Sadie Mae allowed her to choose her own clothes this morning because she just could not muster the strength to get out the warmth of the bed and my arms (I like to think I have that effect on the ladies anyways, especially since they think I look like Luther

Vandross). I figure her problem has to be centered around school.

"Layne and Anne, clean off that table and go outside to play."

"Can we get our bikes out of the garage?" pipes up Layne, who is excited to go outside.

"I'll think about it," I say quickly. "Just hurry up and go outside for now."

"OK," Layne and Anne say in unison, and they quickly clean the kitchen and run outside, slamming the screen door.

Aliyana

While sitting in my room, listening to Michael Jackson's version of "Smile" from his latest two-disc CD, *HIStory*, I heavily consider what made him sing this song. What does he have to smile about other than his fairytale ranch, personal amusement park and animals, loads of money, and his killer dance moves? He is currently on the verge of a felonious child sexual assault conviction in which he could lose all that he had to smile about except the dance moves, which he would probably later only be able to execute in a box of a prison cell. I look at the pictures in his album book. With all of the public charity events and open displays of love and friendship with a variety of people, he certainly did not seem to be a child molester. If someone asks me, the parents of those boys are only out to get all that he has to smile about, except the dance moves.

But what about me? He is supposed to be my favorite artist, my hero, and my counselor through his music. In this song he is telling me to smile even though I have a breaking and aching heart. Should I still smile with my disgusting overbite and discolored teeth? Smile while the nappy balls, also known as "bee bees," on the back of my neck outrace each other to an invisible finish line? At least Michael has the money to alter his appearance for all of the poor and middle-class critics who want to criticize his nose surgeries. All I have is water that I pray will keep my hair swinging when I wet it.

I blame God. He had the power to give me the golden brown hair of my wealthy, milky-colored peers or the hazel eyes of my biracial friends. Instead, He decided to make me ugly, the butt of every joke in each of my classes, the reason behind the snickers and the laughter. I anxiously crave to be noticed for who I am. If only others could see behind physical flaws, they could see my heart that beats in the same area of the body, in the same fashion as their own, pumping the same color blood.

Pastor Whitaker

"So do you have any homework to do?" I ask.

"Yeah, a little," Aliyana replies in a melancholy tone. She starts to carry her book bag out of the living room as if she is carrying the weight of the world on her shoulders.

"Well, what's wrong? You seem so down," I say in the most understanding, *I am here if you want to talk*, way. I thought that she would respond the way most teenagers respond. And she does.

"Nothing."

"Tell you what. Why don't you go change out of your school clothes into your relaxing clothes? Then, come talk to me about it," I say with a wink of my eye.

"No, I will be fine. Really..."

"Aliyana, just trust me and do as I asked, OK?"

"Yes, sir."

I contemplate how to talk to her. Should I sit across from her or beside her? Maybe I should show her how much I really care and allow her to stretch her long legs over my lap.

Aliyana

Mr. Whitaker seems sincere and is very adamant that I talk to him about my worries. Initially, I questioned why he would care. I figure there is nothing he can do, so why bother? But he was just too persistent. So I cave in. What will it hurt to share my pain? It would be a relief to at least actually talk to someone since my mother does not listen to me.

Overwhelmed with emotion, I hurl, "I am so sick of people talking about me, putting me down!" I begin to cry uncontrollably as Mr. Whitaker eases closer to me on the couch. He uses his hand to wipe warm tears from my eyes. I notice that this gesture is so sweet.

"Who talks about you, Aliyana?"

There is something about the way he asks me that question. Just the fact that he used my name at the end of the question makes me feel identified, belonging to someone or something. What? I do not know. I do know that I am too embarrassed to answer his question, so I do not respond.

Mr. Whitaker anticipates a response. After realizing that I would simply sit and wallow in self-pity, he replies, "You are a beautiful young lady. Don't be intimidated by silliness at your school. Half of those kids are probably jealous of you anyway." "Jealous of what? There is nothing to be jealous of."

"I am sure there are fat people who wish they were your size, dark-skin people who wish they had your skin tone. That kind of silliness you best ignore. You are too good for that."

I soak up the words as freely as a beach towel. I admire him for even addressing things that I actually like about myself. I have stared at myself in the mirror and appreciated the thin build of my body, especially the flatness of my stomach, which does not enlarge even after I consume an extra-large meal.

"You are right," I say, realizing that Mr. Whitaker is still anticipating a response. He seems determined to make me feel comfortable.

"Come here and give me a hug," he says, opening his arms wide. I get off the couch and bend over him to complete the embrace. As his left hand pats my back, I think I feel his right hand graze my buttocks. I stiffen.

"Give me a kiss and then go wash those tears from your face."

Still considering his right hand, I aim to kiss Mr. Whitaker's cheek. He abruptly turns his head so that my kiss lands directly on his freshly moistened lips.

Sadie Mae

I am so sick of Gayle. She just keeps on, what the kids call "player hating." Outside of her constant criticism of what I wear to work, she is now complaining about how I put the boxes on the shelf in the stock room. I have only 20 more minutes of helping her tidy the stock room, and I will be on my way home to see my beloved cousin. I will make it my business tonight to pray for God's intervention with these stressful life situations. I go into the break room to call my mother.

PART 2

"Beware of false prophets,
which come to you in sheep's clothing,
but inwardly they are ravening wolves."

Aliyana

How would others know it is your birthday without you having to announce it? They would see balloons, a cake, streamers, pretty bow-wrapped gifts, and cards with green dead presidents inside. They would hear the laughter of celebrating kids or see faces lit with anticipation while awaiting a piece of a Carvel ice-cream cake. These are the images of others realizing it is your birthday.

I guess this is why no one realized it is my birthday.

While getting dressed this morning, I thought to myself, "Today is my day." Every room I went into, I expected a small gift, card, or trinket of some sort, indicating that someone in this house thought about me. Nothing.

When I went into my mother's room for my daily clothing inspection, I expected her to then hand me a small gift. Nothing but a mere chuckle: "Happy birthday, how old is you today?" So I went to wait at the bus stop, expecting my mother to have my gift, party, or any kind of birthday acknowledgement after school.

My sisters and I are currently at Grandma Ann's house, happy that she has allowed us to switch the channels on her television (birthday acknowledgement from her). When I spotted Grandma Ann's car in the driveway when I was dropped off by the school bus, I knew then that my birthday surprise never existed. However, my hopes rose again right before I walked into Grandma Ann's home. I still expected a party of some sort.

I stare the clock down the entire evening, begging it with my eyes to slow down the time. I cannot bear it to become the next day already without a birthday celebration of some sort. Around 6:30 p.m. the phone rings. I jump in anticipation of a birthday song, dashing across a loveseat and sofa just to answer, "Hello?"

"Hi baby, where's your grandma, huh?" says Ms. Hallie, an elderly woman who lives 10 minutes away and has been my grandmother's buddy for years.

"In the kitchen, cooking."

"OK then, tell her I will call her later, OK?"

"OK," I say, closing not only the phone call but another chance at receiving a birthday wish.

The phone rings again at 8:30 only to be answered by Grandma Ann. She fills the conversation with many active voice phrases like "uh-huh," "hmmm," and "OK." I detect that since she is not talking much and is playing with the phone cord, she has to be talking to my overbearing mother.

Grandma Ann looks up at me, almost with pity, and holds out the yellow receiver. Finally, the phone is for me.

"Hello."

"Happy birthday, again, Aliyana."

Again? I did not have a happy birthday, *again*. "Thanks, Ma."

"Look, I'm not picking ya'll up tonight," she says as my hearts drops and its beat slows. "Ya'll goin' to stay at Alicia's house. There are some Girl Scout cookies on top of the TV I left for you. I was goin' to get you a cake, but you goin' to have to get it later, all right?"

I can barely hold back the tears and sobs, but I manage to disguise this over the phone. "What clothes we goin' to wear tomorrow?"

"I will pick ya'll up tomorrow. You'll have a chance to get some clothes, don't worry about that."

"OK," I say as I hand the phone back to Grandma Ann. I go to the bathroom and shed tears as I have never done before. I feel so hopeless and unwanted. More frequently recently, Mr. Whitaker comes down to our house either on Sunday night or Monday morning and stays until Wednesday. He had to be in town for her to give up my evening of cake. If my mother cannot observe the birthday of her own child due to trying to be under Mr. Whitaker, then what am I worth?

After wiping my tears and cleansing my face, I go back into the living room to watch TV. I remember my mother saying that there were cookies left for me. I look up and snatch the mint-green box of Low-Fat Oat Bars, Girl Scout cookies that taste like they never had any sweetness added to them.

Pastor Whitaker

Leaning back in Sadie Mae's recliner, I ponder having a rendezvous with Kellie Berry. As immature as it may seem, I just cannot view her as a teenager. She seems so much more than that. A woman is beautiful, fully developed, and desired by men. Kellie fills all of these qualifications.

Making love to a woman is fine activity that God has created for men to do. By far, it has been one of my greatest activities: I can gain the trust of a woman by saying "I love you"; I can get a workout by sweating heavy; I can ensure that my diaphragm is efficiently working by regulating a heavy breathing pattern; I can release the daily stresses of life inside of a woman; I can forget that he was the first person to ever touch me sexually.

❖ ❖ ❖

I furiously ran home from school after being terrorized in the hallway and saved by my science teacher. So what that I had on a pink shirt? Whoever made it a law that pink was a girls' color anyway? Would it have made a difference if I told those ignorant pricks that my brother, whom I looked up to and is now deceased, owned this shirt? I frequently question my life and the elements that surround it. I wear my pants around my hips, where they belong, with a belt. Why do they call me gay? I clean my fingernails because I do not want them to be surrounded by dirt. Why do they call me odd? I never teased him back nor hit him. Why did he pick me to touch?

I hated my mother for making me walk home from school through the ghetto to our middle-class neighborhood with my prep school-like attire. I wanted to wear my brother's pink shirt, but not perfectly tucked in with a belt. Dirty men with torn clothes who looked as if they had walked out of Michael Jackson's Thriller video would walk too close to me and ask for change. Sometimes I would run through the neighborhood of evicted families, abandoned homes, and luxury Cadillacs with black tinted windows. Once, I did not run fast enough.

Almost two blocks away from my home, the same boys who harassed me in the hallway were waiting for me at a corner store. They knew that I had to come this way in order to go home. An old, dirty, and bent-over man was with them.

"There he is!" one of the boys yelped. I turned on my heels to run in the other direction, but I was surrounded by other boys I had seen at school.

"OK man, give me my 20 bucks. We gave you your dude."

The old man handed over a crumbled and hardly recognizable $20 bill to the leader of the group. He examined his money, then signaled the other boys to follow him.

I wrestled the old man, thinking I could just knock him down and run. But this dirty old man was not weak. He pushed me up against a wall, unzipped his pants, and began to give me orders.

❖ ❖ ❖

I'm starting to wish I had driven my own car. While listening to the continuous play of gospel music on Heaven 1200 radio, I am also subjected to listening to the continuous play of Daniel, my assistant pastor, who was kind enough to make this trip and drive me in my car. But, I have to be honest, if it was not him, it would have been someone else. Members of the church fall at my feet to serve me.

"That service on Wednesday night was something else there, Pastor Whitaker," Daniel exclaims.

"Yes, Brother Daniel," I reply.

"That's right there, Pastor, you was preaching that Word! How long you been preaching, sir? Oh, that's right. Didn't you say since about eight years now? You was preaching when you was a lil' kid, huh? Yeah, I remember your mama comin' to church and saying that."

"Yes, Brother Daniel," I repeat.

"You let me know if you think I am talking too much, Pastor, cuz I need to talk while I'm driving. It helps me stay awake and all that."

"You're fine, I'm just enjoying the scenery," I say. Lord, this is definitely going to be a long trip.

"You know, Pastor, God is so good. God has blessed not only you, but he blesses me too. You know, me and my wife, we about to have our fourth child."

"Yes, God truly blessed you. Four kids?"

"Yes sir, Pastor. You know the Bible says to be fruitful and multiply. We sho' is multiplying," Daniel says with a chuckle. "When you think you gonna have some kids, Pastor? I mean, you know, when you think you gettin' married?"

"You know, when the Lord is ready for me. He just has to bring the right woman my way."

"What about that gal you got down there in New Bern?"

"Um, well... you know. Still praying on what the Lord wants."

"Oh, OK, Pastor, that's what you supposed to do, you know. Let God lead you."

"That's right, Daniel. Let go and let God."

"You know, Pastor, I'm just so thankful. What kind of man is God? It just makes you wonder and think. God wants us to be free from sin, so He dies for us? I mean, by dying, he made a way for us to live. Could you imagine doing something that strong for anybody, a nation of people?" James Cleveland's "I Don't Feel No Ways Tired" comes on the radio. I begin to hum to one of my favorite gospel songs as I ponder the response to this question, paying attention to the road, reflecting on myself.

"The problem is," I reply after a few seconds of humming, "is that we are not all free from sin. Some people still... sin."

"That's right, Pastor. Some people have not fully sought after God. They have not fully seen the goodness of the Lord and asked Him for His mercy. They are still living their own lives, doing what they wanna do."

"Well, you know, it can be hard for some to see God in the problems that they are facing," I say, thinking about my own weakness. As a matter of fact, prior to Daniel making that statement, I was thinking about seeing Kellie Berry on this trip.

What kind of God, I wonder, would make me feel and believe that I am destined to be called to preach His word, but then give me such a huge weakness for young girls? God has crossed my mind so often. Yes, I am able to dissect I Corinthians 5:17 as if it was a fourth-grade science project frog being dissected by a high school senior. I can explain the Word and the scriptures, not only to couples and individuals, but also to a congregation of people. I just find it so hard to understand why God would give me this gift along with the weakness. Why is it that I can't stop thinking of sexual acts and young women, their smooth, tight bodies, and what I can do with them? I did not even receive this weakness until I became a pastor. I often wonder if this is something that God put into my life to see if I was going to fall for it. Well, I did. How do I get back out of this hole?

"...you know what I mean, Pastor?"

At that moment, I realize that I missed about 15 minutes of Daniel's conversation.

"I think I am going to take a nap now," I say.

"All right then, Pastor. We will be there in another hour or so."

Aliyana

My mother is the hardest person in the world to talk to. Just to get her to see me is like pulling teeth. If I walk into the room, the only thing she has to say to me, if she acknowledges me at all, is what room or area in the house to clean. Sometimes I just wish that as I was walking into the room she would gaze upon me and realize that I am a young lady turning into a woman who needs a woman to advise her on how to do certain things in life. I mean, this school year, I have been in a large Christmas concert and a small ensemble we did for a retirement home. I look into the audience of parents and community members, and the only face that I remember seeing is that of my Aunt Melody, who graciously not only attended the concert, but brought me there and took me home. I was determined to get my mother to attend the spring concert, the final performance of the school year. Not just so she could be sitting in the audience, but so she would have a reason to be proud of me. After so often feeling like there was nothing I did that pleased her, I just wanted so badly to show her that I was good at something.

My plan was to have the house already clean when she came home from work so she would not have a reason to be angry. I would also ask her if she wanted something to drink and bring it to her without being asked.

When she came into the house, she noticed that I cleaned. "Oh, it looks and smells nice in here, Aliyana. Did you use up all my Pine Sol?"

"No, Ma. I didn't. I just put a little bit in some water and used it to clean the whole house."

"You better not had used no dirty water when you cleaned my tables and stuff off."

"I didn't, Ma, I used Windex on the glass and dishwashing liquid for the kitchen table," I say, almost mumbling in disappointment.

"All right now, it looks nice," she says as she goes into her room and closes the door behind her.

I pace around my bedroom. When would be the right time?

I go and knock on her door. No response. I knock again. "Wha' chu want?"

"Do you want something to drink, Ma?"

"No, move away from my door. I'll let you know if I want something to drink."

Now I'm worried. Did I agitate her? Is my opportunity to ask her messed up? I need to just leave her alone just a little while longer and then ask. So I go into the living room to watch television, trying to pass the time away, waiting for the right moment again. She comes out of her room 45 minutes later, seeking her own drink.

"You did your homework?"

"Yes, Ma."

I work up enough courage, "Hey Ma, I know I asked you this already, but I am singing a solo in the upcoming Spring Concert..."

"Didn't I tell you not to ask me about that no more?"

"Well, the choir teacher said..."

"I already told you I don't know what I gotta do that day now. I may have to work. I ain't stressing myself out over no singing."

I am not asking her to stress herself out; I don't want her to be stressed at all. I want her to see me.

I look into my mother's face as she is telling me off and telling me no. She is so beautiful. I sometimes just want to touch her skin, caress her cheek, maybe play with her hair and comb it for her. I would like to roll it up in rollers and comb out her curls. But she does not even want to be touched, not by me anyway. What did

I ever do that would make her want to treat me like this? I feel like an old dusty plant in the corner: good to look at when necessary, dust it off sometimes, then put it back and ignore it.

Sometimes I just figure I don't measure up. She is beautiful, with almond-shaped brown eyes, smooth skin, and dark hair. Me, I am the ugly duckling. Smooth skin but with frequent outbreaks. Long hair but extra kinky and coarse. And, of course, my jacked-up and discolored buckteeth are a sore sight. I figure maybe she sees me as something she cannot believe came from her.

Pastor Whitaker

I wake to hear Daniel laughing hysterically. "What's going on?" I ask.

After gaining his composure, he says, "God, I have never heard anyone snore as loud as you. You must have had a good dream, you were mumbling something."

Actually, I did. I dreamed of Kellie. Her smooth, brown skin connected with mine in a bedroom full of rose-scented Yankee candles and satin sheets. I do not want to seduce her; I want her to seduce me, which is exactly what happened in the dream.

We pull up to a building that resembles a cottage. We are welcomed by a large, hand-painted sign: "Welcome to the Youth Retreat!" There are so many cars that many are parked along the road, which is bordered by trees. There will definitely be a lot of young people here this weekend.

I can't wait to see Kellie.

Sadie Mae

I call C.J. after not hearing from him for two days. I just do not understand why he comes into my house, spends a weekend of passion and love with me, and then goes home and seems to forget that I exist.

"How you doin', C.J.?"

"I am fine, Sadie Mae. You?"

"I was lookin' for you to call me..."

"You know I left yesterday for the Youth Retreat. I had a long trip, then had to preach last night.

I am so embarrassed. "I forgot about your trip. I am sorry; I thought you were at home."

"Nope, I am here. I have to preach again this afternoon, then they have games and activities for the rest of the day."

"Oh, OK. You know them people on my job are really something," I say, relieved to finally have the opportunity to talk to C.J. I begin to explain to him all of the unnecessary comments hurled at me from the other employees and how they treat me in the stockroom. I admit feelings of guilt... maybe I was dressing up a little too much. I mean, it was not necessary to wear suits to work that I wore to church. I also admit to C.J. that I have become anti-social with the other employees over time. After working with them for so long and realizing that they are only out to hurt me, I figure I should just keep to myself. Now I only converse with them in front of other employees and when I have to say something to them in the stockroom. They call me stuck-up and bourgeois. At first, I did not care; it was like a compliment for them to think that I thought I was above them. But now it pains me because it seems that it is all of the staff versus me. I never thought I would admit all of this, but I figure I should at least tell someone how I really feel, just to ease my conscience and hear sound advice if necessary. However, after going on and on about how I feel, I realize that I am doing a lot of talking and C.J. is doing a lot of listening. Or is he?

"C.J., what do you think?"

"What do I think of what?" C.J. responds, sounding startled.

"Of what I just said."

"I apologize, Sadie Mae. I am so tired from all of the activities going on today ..."

I wonder, just how much energy could he have used up on preaching, an activity he does so frequently and usually with little preparation?

Pastor Whitaker

Masturbation. An activity that consumes hours of my days on earth. Some call it a sin; I call it a sinner's blessing and way to paradise. Without fornicating, a sinner can still enjoy the pleasures shared between two people. The power of my hand, Vaseline, and an erotic, late-night HBO signature movie helps with the woes and pressures of being unmarried. Pleasing myself is an act that makes me feel like I do not need marriage—better yet, need a woman—to please me … until ejaculation. Then, I realize it would be pleasant to actually have that physical contact with a curvaceous and voluptuous black woman.

I come close to the end of my activity and realize at the sound of Sadie Mae's voice that I did not hear a word she just said before she asked for my opinion.

"C.J., what do you think?" she asks.

"What do I think of what?" I respond, angry that my fast-driving car is now slowing down as it approaches the finish line. I hate distractions.

"Of what I just said," Sadie Mae replies with a hint of frustration in her voice.

"I apologize, Sadie Mae. I am so tired from all of the activities going on today..."

"Oh, all right then. I will let you go. Will you call me tomorrow?"

"Yeah," I say with a throaty, Barry White sound. I quickly say good night and hang up. I increase the sound on the television just enough so that I can hear the grunts and moans of the actor and actress showing each other around, through, and downtown on their bodies. After reaching my climax, I throw my head back on the pillow and bask in the aftermath, then doze off, while semen dries in my hand.

Hard knocks at the door wake me from what seemed like a 10-minute nap, but was actually an hour and a half. I jump up to open the door and recognize that I am naked. I look through the cabin peephole to see Daniel and partially open the door.

"Pastor, everybody was looking for ya during the youth games and stuff. I told 'em I would check on ya. You sleep?"

"Not now," I say, holding on to the door with one hand and rubbing my head with the other. This is when I see flakes falling from my head, but it is not dandruff. I quickly put my right hand, with the dried semen, behind me.

"You can go back to sleep, Pastor, if you want to. I will just let the others know that you are tired."

"No, I am fine, Daniel. Just give me a few minutes to get myself together, and I will come out. Thanks for coming by."

"No problem, Pastor."

❖ ❖ ❖

Everything is going on. "CHRISTO" instead of BINGO. "Heavenopoly" instead of Monopoly. "Babel" instead of Scrabble. Church members were even creative enough to create a large sign that read, "We did not come here to play around, but to PRAY around!" I think I came to *lay* around. But, as the pastor, I have to make my presence known. I play a few games of checkers and rounds of Bible Trivia, during which all of the youth complain that it is not fair for them to go against and lose to an "expert." So I walk around and converse with some of the parents, especially the single mothers. Single mothers cannot resist me because they all have a goal of becoming the first lady of the church. I become bored with them all except for one mother who wore her church youth retreat T-shirt with a short skirt instead of the baggy "I have to present myself as holy" pants. The other mothers who have these pants on look at her in disgust because of the attention she gets from me. While she rants about how the youth need to stop listening to rap music, I spot Kellie Berry. I excuse myself and seek the attention of the young girl.

She is sitting alone (perfect), attempting to complete a watercolor painting. It looks like someone popped a piece of bubble gum across the canvas, and she sprinkled green hearts on the inside.

"So, what do you call this?" I ask, loud enough for others to hear the conversation so that no one would suspect my intentions.

"This is the design I want on my prom dress," she replies through glossy lips. The word "prom" sets me back a moment. *This girl is still in high school.*

"It's pretty," I say, wondering where to take this conversation next.

"Mr. Whitaker, can I ask you something?" she says, drawing closer to me. I can feel her cool breath, the scent of Icebreaker gum, on my lips. It feels more personal and reassuring that she refers to me as "Mr." instead of "Pastor".

"There was this boy at school..." As she begins to speak, I begin to bulge inside my pants. I am hoping she will admit her sexual desires or acts with this boy and ask for my advice. Instead, she explains that she really liked him, but then he dumped her for another girl.

"I am having such a hard time getting over it. It is all that I think about. It is probably the reason why I have been over here by myself all day. Does this sound weird or crazy?"

The clouds cover the sun and dim the shine that lit Kellie's face. "I think you are just fine. It happens all the time. It was your first heartbreak. But, maybe you two will get back together later. What do you think?"

"Naw, I think I messed that up too," she says, unable to look at me.

"Why?"

She pauses, then sighs long and hard. "Kids at school call me a slut and a tramp because of my a— my butt."

"Were you going to say 'ass'?"

Kellie looks around to see if anyone can hear the conversation, then looks at me with surprise. "I'm sorry. I did not mean to..." As the sun continues to bear down on us, a sudden breeze, feeling cool against my newly suntanned legs, rushes through the park. It reminds me that we are not the only two here. I was listening so intently to Kellie that I felt it was just her and myself. I shield my eyes with my hands from the burning sun.

"It's OK. This is between you and I. Only you and me. I will not tell a soul."

"Thanks, because I don't want my mother to know about the boy and what the kids say. I figured I could trust you."

"Yes, you can trust me."

"Can I trust you with something else?"

Now, swelling with an almost painful feeling of needing to unzip my pants, I adjust how I sit so that I can respond to her sweetly, "Anything, Kellie."

"He asked me to... you know," she says, nodding her head toward my groin, "you know, suck something."

The conversation is almost too much for me to take. I was not expecting this, but damn sure did not want it to end.

"You want to talk in private?"

"Yeah."

❖ ❖ ❖

I allowed Kellie the opportunity to get everything off of her chest while sitting on my bed. She was comfortable enough to admit that she did not want his dirt or urine in her mouth because she believed that high school boys did not clean themselves the way they were supposed to, especially her ex-boyfriend, who would leave immediately after football practice without showering. In addition, she had never done it before.

I watched the clock. In about three hours, the activities would end. I knew I would be fine if I could get Kellie back out there in an hour and a half. I sit before Kellie on the floor on my knees. "Do you trust me?" I ask.

"Yeah, I ain't got a reason not to," she responds, completely naïve to the fact that a grown man should not have his face inches from her private area. She smells of wild berries and watermelon.

"Do you want me to help you so that you will be ready when you meet the right guy?"

"I don't care," she replies through shiny, plump lips. I am aching to pleasure her.

"You remember when you said you did not want me to share with anyone, like your mom, what we talked about earlier?"

"Yes," she replies, still innocent to my intentions.

"There is something I want you to keep between you and me," I say as I kiss her inner thighs. She moans and looks down at me with a yearning for me not to stop what I started. "Yes, it will stay between us," she replies.

I continue to kiss her thighs, getting closer and closer to her private spot. I lift my head, gently pulling up her church T-shirt. I am surprised to find that she is not wearing a bra. Even more excited, I take her small, dark nipples in my mouth. Out of nervousness,

I glance at the door to ensure that it is locked. Then I pull down my pants and underwear.

I ask Kellie, "Do you want me to show you how to do it?"

"No, just let me try..." she says as she bends over and inspects the area. She observes, sniffs, and licks the area until she feels comfortable enough to take all of me into her mouth.

She begins to move faster upon me. I move her away to keep myself from exploding in her mouth. I cannot take too much more of this fire between us.

"It's not bad..." Kellie begins to say. I lie on top of her and pull down her skirt and underwear. I whisper in her ear to tell me if what I am about to do hurts her. She shakes her head to show that she understands. I wonder if this is the same as consent.

I slowly push inside of her. She groans initially and then moans with satisfaction. I feel like a child with unlimited access to ice cream. I can do what I want with her for the next hour and a half. It is only after I begin to move inside her that I realize why the kids at school call her promiscuous.

She is not a virgin.

Sadie Mae

I am sick and tired, tired and sick of telling those kids to get up and get ready for church every single Sunday. They know what today is, and they know what they are supposed to do. I don't understand why I have to beg them to get up, tell them to put a slip under their dresses, and tell them to hide the holes in their stockings. I also tell them what to wear to church, but that is because I don't want my children walking out of the house looking any kind of way. This is why I spend a lot of money on keeping their church clothes looking good.

Aliyana, Layne, and Anne each have about five or six dresses that I bought from a boutique. They either have eyelet lace patterns of flowers or a delicate material. I bought white, yellow, and pink dresses and a shimmery pink raincoat for the summer and spring. They have black, navy blue, and red dresses and a red and black velvet coat for the winter and fall. I especially like the velvet coats because they have matching berets, and they look adorable when they are dressed alike in them.

Despite my excitement about my great taste in clothing, I always have to fight with Aliyana, who almost cries about being dressed like her sisters. She keeps wailing about how she is a teenager and how she should look different from them. That is the problem with families today: there is no unity.

I remember growing up and my mother trying to create unity in the family. Melody was rebellious and ran away to New York. I naively left home at 16 trying to be cute, believing I would be happily married to Richard. The only two of my siblings that stayed behind were Alicia and Arthur Junior. There is so much dysfunction in the family. Today, Melody thinks that because she is the oldest, she is in charge of everything. I get tired of being told what to do by my siblings because I made a stupid mistake with Richard. Alicia and Arthur Jr. get along with each other just fine.

Because it is unpleasantly cold outside, and we are recovering from what threatened to become like a snowstorm but was actually a dusting, I tell the girls to wear their black velvet dresses with the matching coats and berets. I will also wear red and black to look coordinated with my children.

I don't care how Aliyana feels. All three of my children need to stick together and look out for each other. In order to form that bond between the three, it is my job to ensure that they know they are all the same. I am tired of all of this talk about "teenage" this and "teenager" that. As long as Aliyana lives in my house, she will always be a child, and I will always be the adult.

Pastor Whitaker

I am awakened again by a hard knocking on the thick wooden door. It takes me a moment to remember that I am not at home but on the church youth retreat. Then, I remember Kellie.

I call for the person knocking to hold on a moment. I slide on a pair of shorts. I am still wearing the church T-shirt since putting it on earlier to meet and greet. *Kellie.*

A fist pounds at my door again, this time louder and harder. Who would want to knock on natural wood doors that hard? I call out for the knocker to identify himself.

"It's Daniel, Pastor. And it's urgent that I speak with you, please," he says with nervous hesitation. My heart sinks. *Kellie promised she would not tell. Did she?*

"I am coming, Daniel. Just trying to put on some clothes." After I say this, I hear a mumbling. Is Daniel saying something?

I open the door to the wide-eyed Daniel, who has his summer straw hat resting on his stomach. His head is bowed, and he does not look up when I open the door.

"What's going on, Daniel?" I say. I notice that there are a few people standing in the shadows, watching my exchange with Daniel. It is too quiet outside for church youth activities. *This cannot be about Kellie, can it? I knew I should not have trusted a teenager, even if she did give me her word.*

"Pastor, may I come in, please?" he says, sounding choked. I step out of the way and allow him to come into my cottage. Daniel hastily walks in and stands in a corner.

"Please, sit down Daniel," I say, motioning him to a desk.

"I can't, Pastor. I was sent here to tell you that Ms. Berry knows what happened to her little girl..." I have no clue how to respond. After a brief pause, I finally ask, "Well, what happened to her?"

Daniel does not respond nor look at me.

"Daniel?"

"Pastor, you know what happened. I know you don't want me to sit here and describe it for you," he says. "Apparently, Kellie told one of her girlfriends, who told her mother, who told Ms. Berry."

I was in denial. How could she tell someone so quickly? It just happened a couple of hours ago. I remember caressing her smooth, fruit-scented skin. I suddenly feel betrayed. After I counseled her and helped her with her problem, which I kept in confidence, how could she be disloyal to me? I reflect on pulling down her pink and green thong that said "Girlz Rule." The thought that she shared our secret disgusts me.

"I don't know what she could have told her friend. She came to me for counsel and that's it."

"That's it?"

"That's it."

❖ ❖ ❖

The women's choir seemed somewhat tired and drowsy today. The baritone voices had long faces and wrinkled burgundy and gold robes. As a matter of fact, the entire church was solemn today. It was my fault.

I did everything in my power to save myself from further embarrassment. I sat in my office until the last stanza of the choir's song prior to the sermon. While waiting for them to finish their rendition of "Lift Up Your Heads," I had my head down, determined not to make eye contact with anyone. The seat for the pastor was directly behind the podium, so I avoided moving to either side to keep my face from view of the seemingly angry congregation.

I felt that at any moment someone would jump up and scream in anguish, further making me feel as if I should crawl into a hole and die. I wished someone would just shoot me and help to end this misery.

Kellie Berry and her mother did not show up today. Minister Daniel only said, "Praise the Lord," and has said nothing since. However, he did leave a note in my office, on top of a few empty boxes, saying:

Pastor Whitaker,

I am praying for you. God can heal and deliver. I found these for you to put your stuff in.

As the choir reaches the end of the chorus, I feel nauseated, my heart pounds, and I am almost breathless. The palms of my hands became sweaty and I feel a rush of anxiety. I realize I will not be able to speak to this audience who once cheered at my every stomp, but is now simply sitting and fanning themselves, wordless.

A sister from the church, dressed as if she is supporting breast cancer awareness in a bubblegum pink suit with a matching hat and shoes, comes to the podium to read the announcements. As I admire her well-coordinated attire, her eyes catch mine, reading, *how could you?* I quickly look away, suddenly wondering what she will say to the congregation during announcements. I decide that if anything is said directly about me, I will simply walk out and away from the church, as I planned to do anyway after addressing the congregation.

The sister in the pink suit begins to read from several different sheets of paper.

"The announcements for today are..." she says as she fumbles through what seems to be 10 sheets of paper, "Bible study and prayer service this week are cancelled..." She stops speaking and puts her head down. While we all wait for her to continue, I see her shoulders rapidly moving up and down. A choir member comes down from the choir stand to help her to her seat. A different choir member comes down to the podium to help move the service along. *Thank God.*

As she walks toward me, I reminisce on all of the times she came to my office for help. Whenever she had a dispute with the choir director, her husband, or her oldest son, who is now in jail, she came to me for prayer. I look at the floor as she approaches to avoid another feeling of betrayal. She announces that the choir will sing again, prior to the sermon. This statement causes a murmur throughout the church.

The choir member then says, "So what do you want? Do you want the sermon *now*?" She says the word "now" as if they should not want to hear a sermon, especially after what I did.

She continues, "You know what, saints, church people, children of God, it seems as if you want bloodshed today. Everybody makes mistakes, and that is all I am saying." As she finishes, the low murmurs suddenly turn into the angry sounds of quick movement in the pews, as several congregation members get up and walk out of the church, holding their children's hands.

The choir member goes back to her seat with the angry choir members. She sits down, and after a few moments, I realize they are not going to sing. I stand. The church becomes silent.

I put on my glasses and turn on the podium lamp. I guess they think I am going to preach because the low murmurs begin again. Then it becomes silent. All I can hear is the squeaking of old wood under my feet. All I can feel is sweat on my chest and inside the palms of my hands. Fear suddenly consumes me, and I imagine just running out of the church and never looking back.

I begin, "Because of matters at hand, I will not deliver the Word of the Lord today. I will also be..." I choke. "I'll be stepping down as the pastor. I would rather resign than be condemned by those who do not know or understand my situation. Today, Assistant Pastor Daniel will preach." As Daniel walks up to the podium in his purple and gold silken robe, I proceed to walk out of the sanctuary and toward the pastor's study. I pretend not to hear clapping from the congregation, a signal that they agree with my departure.

Aliyana

Layne, Anne, and I have about six or seven of the exact same dresses that Mommy bought from what seemed to be an out-of-style, abandoned bridal shop. The dresses, or "pretty rags," as I call them, either have lacy patterns of flowers or a silky, see-through material. Mommy acted like they were the last dresses available on the planet by buying them in all the colors available: white, yellow, and pink. She even bought us matching pink raincoats for the summer and spring. In addition, my sisters and I have matching black, navy blue, and red dresses and a red and black velvet coat for cold weather. I especially hate the velvet coats because they have matching berets, and it seems that every Sunday we are dressed alike in them. Those are the Sundays Mommy wants to go to the mall.

Mommy's horrific taste in clothing causes us to argue constantly. Well, maybe it is more like she is arguing at me, and I am not allowed to voice my opinion about how hard it is being a teenager, looking just like my elementary and middle school sisters. So I simply pout or become withdrawn.

Mommy keeps wailing about how families today have no unity. How can she teach me about unity through wearing Cinderella-like clothing when she could not stay unified to my dad, and she was wearing a gold ring?

At this stage in the game, I feel defeated. Being in a high school is the same as being in a fashion show; as soon as anyone walks onto the stage (into the school) at 8:30 a.m., everybody stands up against the walls to watch them walk down the long, narrow runway (hallway). Then again, at lunch, everybody receives a second chance to be gawked at, as if there had been a clothing or scene change in one of the classrooms.

Caucasian kids who live in trailers or older homes tell me I look pretty. *Liars.* Caucasians who are considered "preps" and live in homes that we cannot see from the roads do not acknowledge me. *Snobs.* Black kids who live in the projects tease me whether I look good or bad. *Dummies.* Blacks who have parents with money side with the snobs. *Phonies.*

I want so badly to fit in with one group. I would honestly prefer to become a hit amongst the snobs, but I do not have the money nor the beauty to even begin to fit in with them. The snobs have straight, white teeth, while mine are stained and crooked. The snobs have brand-new convertibles and BMWs in the student parking lot from their parents, while I cannot even get my driving permit. The snobs have bright-colored, embroidered L.L. Bean book bags, while I have a masculine Payless book bag. The snobs have healthy, long hair, which they brush throughout each class period while I gawk in envy. My hair is thin, brittle, dry, and usually poorly concealed with a self-done weave. The snobs seem happy as they walk past my loneliness in the hallway. I can smell the sweet chamomile and lavender fragrances of their perfumes as they stroll through the hall with their bouncy-haired, football-player boyfriends. I imagine that if they always look and smell nice and appear to be happy, they must have mothers who are waiting for them in estates with Andes mints and hot cocoa. They must have bedrooms the size of our house. In front of blazing fireplaces with their moms, who are overly concerned about their well-being, the snobs must receive long hugs and daily chats about their perfect grades in school. I long to experience this type of life.

The group that I actually fit into is the group of liars, which is best for me because it keeps me from going into a bathroom stall and dipping my head into a toilet. They lie to me; I lie to them. We tell each other that we are the smartest and best dressed, knowing we are outdone by the snobs.

While we may not be all that we think we are, we do know that no matter how frequently the dummies put us down, we do look better than them. They attempt to appear "hard," dressed as if they just walked off the set of a rap video. The girls wear shirts too small for them that expose their belly buttons and developing breasts. Since the new fad is to be woman enough to wear thongs, they make sure those show at the top of their tight, breath-cutting jeans. And I do not have to have a brother to see a pair of boxer shorts; they are exposed on the behind of almost every black boy dummy. The boys wear oversized football starter jackets and oversized T-shirts.

It always amazes me how much the dummies can expose their body parts, but they cannot expose any intelligence. The dummies keep our master-degreed teachers in anxiety by constantly disrupting classes. Also, they always seem to have the need to show how well they can fight, which they will do at the drop of a hat. One time, I witnessed a dummy beating up a snob boy because "the prep kid think he smart," the dummy exclaimed as he was taken away in handcuffs. The snob kid's parents pressed charges against the dummy kid, so I never saw the dummy again.

Because it is horribly cold outside today, and we are recuperating from the recent dusting of snow, Mommy told us to wear the black velvet dress with the matching coat and beret. An hour later, she proudly walks out of her bedroom, wearing a classy, sequin-embellished red and black suit.

I constantly complain about being treated like a child, with good reasons. I am not all that bothered by this since the people in our church are elderly and think we look "adorable." But when Mommy starts talking about going to places other than church in these hideous and frilly garments, then I catch a serious attitude.

A teenager should be able to go to the movies, or mall, or just to the library with other teenagers. I cannot go anywhere without my sisters. I feel like if I could just make it to the door, I would start running. I would keep running and never look back. As long as I live in Mommy's house, she will always be the adult, and I will always be seen as a child instead of the young, pretty ugly woman I am slowly growing into.

Sadie Mae

The women in the church feel so threatened by my presence. I mean, is it my fault that I keep myself and my children looking superior? Besides, they don't know what I have been through.

As we walk up the steps to the church, I notice that the ushers glance at each other and then look back at me and my children. I instantly feel a need to straighten up my posture and smile. If they are going to stare and talk about us, I am going to give them something good to look at.

I look back to make sure my children are standing up straight. Anne catches my eyes and wants to hold my hand. I don't refuse because of my attentive audience. I hold her hand with my left hand and make sure that my matching red clutch is seen in my right hand with the sequin side showing. Layne walks the strange walk that she always has. Aliyana looks as if she is disturbed, probably because she did not want to wear the church clothes. I angrily whisper to Layne and Aliyana for them to stand up straight and walk. We walk past the ushers, who hand the brochure to Aliyana instead of handing it to me.

Later, I call C.J. to tell him about the Sunday service. I tell him about the rudeness of the ushers; in addition to not wanting to give me a program, they also passed by my pew when distributing the paper church fans on wooden sticks. Also, plenty of women were staring at me in church: women with kids, women who wished they had kids, women who had kids and a husband. The jealousy in their eyes caught my eye every time I looked around the church. Even when I looked straight ahead, women would either walk by to look at me or turn around in their pews.

I also tell C.J. about the friendliness of the pastor. He seemed to watch over me from the pulpit, as if he was using his gaze to attempt to keep me safe from all the animosity of the jealous women around me. After church, while gently shaking my hand, he gave me several compliments on our neat and "regal" appearance. The warmth of his hands and in his eyes made me feel surrounded with peace, safety, and a man's undying and blameless love.

All C.J. has to say is, "Um-huh."

"Are you listening? I don't even know if I should continue going to the church because while the pastor likes me, the women there surely don't."

"That's your choice, Sadie. That's a choice that only you can make. "

Then C.J., silent for a few moments, finally says, "I will be there tomorrow. I am leaving tonight."

"Oh, you don't have night service at your church?" I ask.

"I will no longer be at this church. As of today, I stepped down," he says in a monotone voice, as if he does not want to continue the conversation. However, I am confused. This never came up in conversation before.

"Why? What hap—"

"Sadie," he says, cutting me off hastily, "there are some issues at the church that need to be resolved, and I just did not want to be a part of it anymore. That is all. I will be finding another church soon."

"OK," I say before we abruptly end the conversation. As I go to sleep, I think about C.J. giving his final sermon at the church, the shock of the congregation, and each member embracing him in love before he leaves. Just in case he is feeling down about the situation, I will have to ensure that he feels welcome in my home tomorrow.

Aliyana

My bus driver drives past my house in order to turn around at the end of the narrow, North Carolina road. As we drive past my house, I realize that Mr. Whitaker is visiting when I see his Cadillac sitting in the driveway. When I get off the bus, I find Layne and Anne playing outside, happily riding their bikes up and down our back road. It is warmer today than it has been, with the occasional brisk breeze slapping my sisters' faces through cries of excitement to each other. The trees behind the house sway and rock while the leaves whisper harsh messages to the world. While my sisters are enjoying the warm weather, I hurry inside, feeling the chill.

Used to seeing Mr. Whitaker sitting in my mother's house, I say hi and walk past him and the television to go to my bedroom. As I change out of my horrendous, oversized athletic T-shirt and jeans, I hear Mr. Whitaker yell down the hall.

"How was school today?" he asks.

"Fine," I yell back, and continue to change.

"Everything went all right?" he asks, this time sounding as if he is walking down the hallway.

"The kids got on my nerves, but other than that, it was fine," I say, pushing the door closed.

"You looked a little upset when you came in today..." he says, sounding as if he is right outside my door.

"Uh, yeah. I was. I'll get over it though," I say quickly so that he can go away. But he continues.

"When you come out, your mother said she has some food in the fridge she wants you to heat up for all of you to eat. I think she said it was some leftover Hamburger Helper."

"OK, I will," I say, feeling relieved to hear him walking away from my bedroom door. Couldn't he have just waited until I came out to say that? That was weird, but I dismiss it.

I look in the mirror at my hair. There is no way I can go to school tomorrow with it looking this frizzy. I asked my mother to allow me to get a perm. She furiously replied, "Hell no!" as if my hair was her hair. I already know that I cannot talk to her about pressing issues, but all I asked for was the straightening of my hair, not a car and a boyfriend. Because of her lack of attention to detail and to my feelings, I am getting teased at school. It just isn't fair.

Pastor Whitaker

My heart goes out to Aliyana. She really is such a beautiful girl: tall, statuesque, and evenly caramel-colored—just like her mother. The defined bone structure of her face is set behind two sparkling, dark eyes, even if they are hidden behind a pair of thick spectacles. She has plump lips and a strong jawline. A long neck connects her lovely head to her long, slender body. Of course, it seems as if she is unattractive due to the mess her mother makes her wear outside of church clothes. However, with the right makeover, Aliyana could be a supermodel.

I figure I should be the one who uplifts her spirits and helps her understand the true and natural beauty that she is. I consider all of the compliments I could give, but they have to be appropriate, right? The girl is only 14 years old—or is it 15? Either way, she should have a man in her life now showing and telling her that she is a goddess. If her father is not here to do it, then I can certainly fulfill this role as... well, a member of the family.

My mind wanders to thoughts of Kellie Berry. Such a beautiful girl, but both she and her mother were severely misguided. The missing ingredient in these situations is the same—a man.

I believe that my thoughts and feelings are biblical. God made man to be a caregiver of the earth and all that was included on earth. Men are to protect the environment, the women, and the children. If men fail to see their roles through, then they have failed God.

Sadie Mae

"Aliyana knows better. I have to tell her to wash the dishes, vacuum the floor, help her sisters clean the room, and on and on and on. She just refuses to do this stuff on her own, rolling her eyes and mumbling under her breath whenever I ask her to do something. Well, from now on, I ain't asking—I'm *telling* her what to do because I am sick of her nasty, poor attitude towards cleanliness. It is not enough for her to keep just her side of the room clean. This is family, not an individual living arrangement," I argue.

Valuing C.J.'s opinion, I tell him about Aliyana, despite the fact that it is early in the morning.

"Sadie Mae, leave the girl alone now. At least half of the room is clean. There are many kids who do not even clean their room."

"Well, you don't think it's wrong that I have to tell her what to clean up all the damn time?" I say, annoyed.

C.J. is clearly annoyed too because he turns over in the bed and refuses to respond. Minutes later, he begins snoring. So I get up and make him a breakfast of eggs, bacon, pancakes, and grits. He will listen once I bring him the food.

Pastor Whitaker

I am thoroughly disgusted with Sadie Mae. She is entirely too hard on Aliyana. Granted, I do not have children of my own, but I have seen the effects of an overprotective parent at the church. Kids need to feel that they have some type of freedom, that they can go to the mall with their friends and do fun, age-appropriate activities. Sheesh, Aliyana cannot even go inside the refrigerator for a soda without asking for permission. It is a shame.

I can somewhat understand. Sadie Mae just got out of a domestically violent relationship. I mean, she was battered throughout her marriage, which had to take a toll on her mind in some way. Because of the lack of protection that she had, she probably feels that she has to be the protector of her household. So what is my issue? A woman cannot effectively defend or protect her own house. This has been proven, at least by Sadie Mae, when her outraged and remarkably stupid ex-husband broke into the house a few times. I do not even know or remember the number of times that police came to the house to remove the ex-husband.

We have heard it before—children need their fathers. What about the unfortunate situations where the child has no choice? Aliyana did not choose that her father should leave. I believe that she cares for him a great deal, as much as she talks about him. However, to fill the absence and the void, I feel that I can pick up the slack where her father left off. Otherwise, how will she know how to survive in this strange and male-led world?

Sadie Mae keeps blocking me. Every time I try to take Aliyana under my wing, Sadie has a problem with it. It is as if Sadie is fighting for my attention, which isn't all bad. Most of the time, I am trying to protect Aliyana from Sadie's wrath. Aliyana does not even realize the frequency of my defense of her, but since her dad is gone, I will show her that I've got her back. I plan to make myself more visible and form a better relationship with my family. After all, we all are cousins.

Aliyana

I bury my face so deep within the lace-trimmed, pink satin pillow. I want to cry out so loudly, so badly, but Mommy does not allow me to close my bedroom door, and her bedroom is directly across the hall. If she heard me even whimper, the tirade of yelling from her end will begin again and possibly end with a smack across my face.

I have always wondered why parents smack their children for crying. Don't they realize that this will only cause them to cry harder? Don't they realize that the child will hurt worse? Do they realize that crying is a part of life and being human? I think it is absurd that if I cry, especially if I am already hurting about something else, that I should get smacked, inflicted with more pain, just because my mother deems it necessary.

It just isn't fair. I keep my side of the room clean, and despite all of the problems at home, I keep my grades up. But I get yelled at for not washing dishes, not sweeping the floor. My mother calls me lazy and sloppy, yet my room is cleaner than hers. What gives? What do I have to do to prove myself around here?

I blame God. This is His fault entirely. I begin questioning God as I sob harder, as quietly as I can.

Pastor Whitaker

As a plenipotentiary man of God, ordained to be kind, caring, respectful, and loving to all of God's people, and as the man who baptized Aliyana, I make sure that she knows that I feel the way her mother treats her is wrong.

As I talk to Aliyana, she sits very still with her long fingers intertwining, folding in her lap. She appears 15 pounds heavier than she is due to her oversized clothes. She looks so boyish but acts like a lady. She sits straight up in the seat and blinks with such grace. While her lashes are not long, her large dark brown eyes illuminate my heart when I gaze into them, although she never holds my gaze.

"I do realize that it is hard to be yelled at constantly and put down... especially by your mother, the woman who is supposed to love you unconditionally. You know what I mean?"

"Yeah," Aliyana responds as if she is being lectured to. I do not want her to see me in a threatening way. I am not against her. I love her.

"Aliyana, come here," I softly demand.

"Huh?" She looks at me as if I am speaking Japanese.

"Come and sit beside me. I want you to know how special you are."

When I see her hesitation, I feel that she is probably uncomfortable.

"There is no need for you to be afraid of me. I am not your mother. I am not going to hurt you. I will always be here for you."

She slowly gets up from the love seat and sits beside me, with enough space for a person to sit between us.

"Come here. I am not going to hurt you," I say.

"I can hear you," she replies. "I am sitting beside you." Aliyana chuckles nervously.

I lean over and take her hand in mine. "I love you, Aliyana. Nothing is going to change that. I will always be here for you. There is no need to fear your mother. I will not allow her to hurt you either."

I notice a tear run down Aliyana's cheek. I brush it away, and she begins to sob, heaving so hard that she can barely catch her breath.

I lean in closer to her and wrap my arms around her. She seems to cry even harder. I continue to assure her that she has support.

"I know, baby... it's OK. Go ahead... get it out," I whisper above her head as she sobs into my chest.

I look down to see her head nodding in slow motion.

I remember the day of her baptism. She was so tall and lean for her age. The basin of water was low, and she practically had to bend over completely in order for me to sprinkle the water upon her head. Seeing her body bent over in front of me caused me to feel a rush of excitement in my groin.

I am jerked from my thought when Aliyana tussles to be released from my grip. I do not realize how tight I am hugging her, and I release my arms just enough so that she can look up into my eyes.

"I need to go blow my nose," she mumbles.

"It is OK... go ahead and get it out." Aliyana just lays back on my chest as I continue to hold her shivering body. I see shadows out of the corner of my eye and look out of the living room window to see her sisters coming back to the house on their bicycles. I tell Aliyana to go and clean herself up while I help her sisters put their things away.

"Thank you. I really appreciate it."

"Don't mention it," I reply.

❖ ❖ ❖

I hang up the phone with Sadie Mae, who calls to tell me that she gets off work at 9 p.m. and will be home around 9:30. She asks me if there was anything I need, as she usually does. She never asks about her kids. I tell her that I will stay the night, but I plan to leave in the morning. She begs and pleads with me to stay, knowing that I do not really have to be back home until Wednesday, and today is Monday. I figure Aliyana will need me to mediate her mother's outbursts towards her. I agree to stay.

Anne and Layne greedily eat their Spaghettios, claiming that they are so good. Aliyana washes the dishes behind them so her mother will come home to cleanliness. She continues to look discouraged as she washes the dishes, but I plan to help her feel more at ease before her mother gets home.

As soon as they finish their meal, I make Anne and Layne go to bed.

"Aw, man, it's only 7:30!" Layne attempts to yell at me.

"I don't care, do as I say now!" I yell back so she knows not to ever talk to me like that again.

"What about Aliyana?" Anne asks.

"Aliyana, go put on your night clothes too," I say to her, ignoring Anne altogether.

All the girls go into their bedrooms to get dressed and ready for bed.

❖ ❖ ❖

I watch a bit of the nightly news. There is a report of a tar spill on a highway, a rise in gas prices, and a man who is being charged with first-degree rape of a 12-year-old girl. According to the arrest warrant, he had been raping the girl over the course of nine months.

Rape?

Rape means that the man forced himself on that poor girl. *That poor girl.* I think it is absurd for a man to think that way about a female. They are to be treated with love, touched with gentleness, spoken to tenderly. If only the rapist would have approached the girl differently, they could have had a totally different relationship.

There is nothing wrong with making a lady feel special.

PART 3

"The scab is a traitor to his God,
his mother, and his class"

JACK LONDON

Aliyana

I am so groggy and tired. As far as I know, I am still in my bed. It should be early in the morning because Mommy has not yet awakened me for school, but I hear Anne, I think.

"Aliyana, there's a fire in my room," she calmly says, standing like an apparition beside my bed.

I get up out of the bed and walk over to Layne's bed, turning and pushing her to awaken her. She sits straight up like a zombie, mumbling under her breath at me for disturbing her dreams, and then walks down the hall. I follow Layne out of the room, not thinking to put on a pair of shoes. Immediately to the right, Anne's room is ablaze, with thick and heavy black smoke escaping in my direction.

Sadie Mae

"I ain't asleep," I say as I roll over in my bed, drool spread across my cheek.

"Ma," Anne says, "there's a fire in my room."

"What?" I say groggily, trying to figure out how she got in my room. I usually keep my door locked at night.

"There is a fire in my room," she repeats, and walks out of the room.

I jump out of my bed and grab my purse. As I bend over to put on a pair of shoes, I inhale smoke. I look towards the left side of my room, near the door, and notice a bright light. As I put on my second shoe, I peek towards the ceiling and catch a glimpse of the contaminating cloud that is causing my heavy coughs. I pick up my purse and rapidly dial 911. Thank God they do not ask too many questions. As I exit my room, I hear the windows in Anne's room shattering.

I run out into the hall with my hands over my face, protecting it from the heat of the blaze directly across from me. I begin sobbing uncontrollably as I temporarily stop in the living room thinking of what I should grab.

"Aliyana! Anne! Layne!" I scream. I hope they are not still near that bedroom. I hear crying from outside. Believing the crying comes from my kids, I run out to make sure they are all there.

I see all three of my daughters standing on the porch in front of the house. They are wearing nothing but their pajamas, not even shoes. Through my tears I can barely see my neighbors running in my direction. I begin to cry convulsively. Anne, who is not crying (probably because she is too young to detect how serious this situation is), holds my hand.

"Sadie Mae! Ya aight?" the father of the household next door yells. "Ya gotta move away from the house! *Now!*"

How did this happen? When is the fire department going to get here? I should have grabbed my safe deposit box! I forgot my ring that I just bought!

Aliyana

The neighbor made us stand on the street. My mother began to scream frantically and could not seem to get herself together. If it was not for the man next door, I do not know what would have happened. I am scared. My sisters and I are shivering with almost no clothes on, standing outside without shoes at 2 in the morning, in the chill of the night air. Minutes later, when we begin to hear the sounds of sirens, the large front windows shatter with a boom as if a bomb was set off. A violent, hungry fire devours what was left of our home.

Sadie Mae

I feel that all hope is lost. I am a single mother with three kids, now with no home. What in the world am I supposed to do? Where do I go? What the heck is next?

I stifle my cry as I lie on my mother's couch. With my head buried deep within the cushions, I continue to ask myself question after question about what the future ahead will hold. I attempt to sneak my hand under my eye to wipe away a tear, feeling the cold of gold against my face. I have my 2-carat diamond rings, one on each finger, survivors of the ferocious fire. I was relieved to have put them away in the safety box. What I thought to be a silly habit turned out to mean survival for some of my favorite accessories. I could replace clothes, furniture, even the walls of the house, but the rings were irreplaceable, expensive and mine. I purchased them for myself to show myself that

I love me and that I do not need any man to prove that.

When I went back to the house to try and salvage what I could, I came away with more than I thought I would: my safety deposit box with the rings inside, a few soot-soiled books, smoke-covered shoes, and dishes that just needed a good cleaning. The garage, made of concrete so strong that the smell of smoke did not penetrate it, was basically left unharmed. It was still damp and cold but intact and standing.

I have to figure out what is next for me and my kids. I cannot reside with my mother, who is currently serving us gravy lima beans and bread, for long.

Aliyana

So the day arrives when I can get off the bus at River Bend. My mother left a note for me to catch the bus to an address that I have to get the bus driver to point out to me. Most of the other students got off of the bus already, and I am glad to be one of two students remaining. During the bus ride, I heard the other students whispering about why I was on *their* bus. Before I left school, all of my friends cooed and cawed watching me get on the bus. I was excited to see where this address would lead.

We pass home after home, in a neighborhood bordered by clear lakes and a canal, with yachts resting in their private docking spaces. We couldn't possibly be staying in one of these two- and three-story homes with majestic columns, long driveways, and neatly trimmed yards with such bright green grass. Many homes do not even have closed windows. I can see right through the sunny rooms, grand entrances, and beautifully draped living quarters. I imagine myself living every day in one of these homes. What would it be like to wake up in a room that's the size of a whole apartment, with high ceilings? What would it be like to pass a golf course during an afternoon stroll or go swimming in the back yard? Instead of eating on wooden dinner tables, I imagine that these people eat on marble or granite countertops with bar stools, and polished stainless steel pots hanging securely over their heads. Even the air smells crisp, clear, and free of all of the pollution of a middle-class society. I think about the people who live like this. They must be so calm and at peace. They must be teens who are greeted by their mothers at the door after school. All I can think about is my desire to live like this, but I can only imagine.

The bus comes to a stop in an area that has townhomes, but they are still very much regal in appearance.

"Two-twenty-four is right there, young gal." The bus driver points to the place that will be my home for the next week or so.

As I get off of the bus, I thank God for whatever aid supplied my mother with this opportunity. We were so cramped in Grandma Ann's house. It will be lovely to sleep on a bed instead of a couch.

As I approach the front door, burgundy and freshly painted with a gold knob, I think about our old house. I should have been excited to hear that our home will be rebuilt from scratch, but I just cannot seem to shake the images of the dark, damp, burnt house that we used to call home. It is as if we are abandoning it instead of nourishing it back to health. What in the world could I have done to stop that fire?

The burgundy door begins to open, startling me from my thoughts. It is my mother.

"Aliyana, go in there and fold those clothes up in those boxes. Ya'll just threw 'em in there. Now, that ain't no way to treat no clothes! And make sure you wash those dishes after ya'll eat," she says. I walk past her, pretending that she said nothing, and admire the room.

The living room is large, furnished with a flowered Victorian couch set and deep maple-colored tables. The ceiling is high and sloped, and there is a fireplace, which looks somewhat artificial.

"Aliyana, did you hear me? I get off work at 9. There is some spaghetti in a can in the cabinet or on the counter. Just heat it up! Don't go cooking nothing...I ain't trying to have everything burn down..."

How selfish was that comment? I ignore my mother as she closes the door to leave for work. I follow the voices of Layne and Anne.

"Look, Aliyana! Look at our room!" one of my sisters calls out to me.

Our room, which all three of us must share until our home is built, is not as big as the room in my imagination on the bus. It is small, with three beds, large windows, and a chest and dresser with a hefty mirror. While beautiful, the room seems like a death sentence because I have to share it.

"What are ya'll doing in here?" Pastor Whitaker asks. All of us let out a scream, not knowing he was there or that he came in. How long was he standing in the doorway?

"Cleaning up," Anne replies as she lifts her naked Barbie doll in the air and begins talking for her again.

"Make sure ya'll keep this room clean and don't put any marks on the walls. Don't write on these walls, you hear me?" he says, focusing on Anne and Layne. I guess he figures I know better than to write on walls. "Ya'll get ready to go to bed."

"But it is only 5, and we haven't eaten yet!" I argue. I hate having a sitter. I can watch myself.

"Well, ya'll go eat, and then you are going to bed," Pastor Whitaker says calmly. Anne and Layne walk past him briskly, anxious to eat. I begin to unpack my book bag. I was going to ask him what time did he want me to do my homework since I had to go to bed so early.

"How was school today?" he asks.

"Fine," I reply. He stands in the doorway and continues staring at me. It's eerie. It is as if he has a look of desire in his eyes, for me. I am pretending to look for something in my book bag when he walks up to me, looks behind him, lifts my head with his hand, and kisses me on my mouth. I become very still—is this really happening?

"You are beautiful, Aliyana. Don't worry about those kids at your school."

"Uh-huh." I could not force myself to say any more than this. Pastor Whitaker continues to look me in my eyes.

"I love you," he says, and leaves the room.

❖ ❖ ❖

I lie in the bed and can't sleep, even if I wanted to. The afternoon replayed over and over again in my head. Why did that grown man kiss me like that? Was it harmless or does he like me... like that? I just could not settle the thought in my mind. Was I supposed to kiss him back? What if he tries to kiss me like that in front of my sisters or my mother?

I could hear him and my mother in her bedroom talking. It sounded as if they were talking about the new house and moving in soon. Layne and Anne were asleep, snoring softly.

I began to get sleepy, and my heavy lids started to close. Suddenly, I heard squeaking coming from the bed in my mother's room. Someone was coming.

I closed my eyes quickly and pretended to be asleep. Little did I know that this would be the first of many times I would be pretending.

Someone is walking down the hall. I assume it is Pastor Whitaker because of the heaviness of the footsteps. The footsteps briefly stop at our bedroom door. Even though it is dark, I am sure to keep my eyes closed and my chest heaving. The footsteps continue past the door and into the kitchen. I hear water running. I hear Anne and Layne still snoring, their sleep undisturbed by the passerby.

The footsteps move toward the bedroom door again, this time lightly. It sounds as if the person is trying to be quiet as they walk through the house. The steps stop in front of my door again. My heart begins to beat rapidly as I continue to pretend. My mind flashes back to the kiss from this afternoon. The footsteps enter our bedroom. My heartbeat is so rapid now I feel as if I can hear it. I continue to "sleep." The footsteps stop in the center of the floor. I try to imagine what the person is doing. Is it Mommy checking on us, which she has never done before? Is it Pastor Whitaker checking on us? If so, what in the world is he looking at?

The footsteps start toward my bed. I become nervous, anticipating someone saying my name aloud or something being wrong. I can smell breath—*his* breath. Pastor Whitaker is leaning over me.

Pastor Whitaker

I kneel beside Aliyana's bed. I notice how her long and lean body spills over the bed, with her feet dangling off of the end. She is a woman, all grown up and too big for a twin bed.

I crave the ability to show her how much I care. With a faint light from the moon seeping through the blinds, I attempt to look at her face. Her body naturally rises and falls with a peaceful breathing pattern. I am praying that she can always be this peaceful.

I brush my hand along the side of her face to feel her softness. She stirs but does not awake. I kiss her on her cheek. Still, she sleeps with relaxation that only rest can give.

I pull back the top of the blanket and pull up her T-shirt. She is not wearing a bra. Her breasts are like perfect lemons without the sourness. She smells of peaches from a fruity lotion she uses often, which has softened her unblemished skin. In the dark, with my fingers, I find her nipples taut and raised. It is as if her body is responding to me. I lightly caress the nipple closest to me with my whole mouth, careful and soft enough not to wake her. She still does not stir, but her body seems to stiffen. I wonder if she has awakened but not reacted. I continue to lovingly caress her nipple with my tongue.

Aliyana

I am dumbfounded. *What am I supposed to be doing? Saying? Pastor Whitaker should not be doing this, right?* I am lying here confused because this is the man who just left my mother's bedroom. *Isn't he supposed to be with her?* I feel doubly angry at myself: for pretending to be asleep when I probably should be yelling at him to stop, and for allowing this to happen in the same room where I sleep with my sisters. *What if they wake up?* There is no way I could explain this to any party in the household.

I knew something was wrong when I heard his footsteps stop in front of my door. He kisses my face. It was as if he was coming for me, a shark, swimming efficiently and quietly so as not to alert the naive prey. A shark's prey is in doubt, wondering if the shark is really present and if it is really coming after *them.* Not this creature, beautifully made by God with such splendor and strength. I imagine being one of the little, ugly, possibly even mangled, fish trying to get away from a great shark.

Then, I feel coolness, as the top of the blanket has been pulled back from my chest. I have to keep reminding myself to breathe so that he will think I am asleep. When my shirt is pulled up, I stop breathing. Thoughts run through my mind:

He is about 47 years old. I am 14.

Isn't he my family, if he is my mother's cousin? Is family supposed to be doing this?

Does he plan on praying when he goes back to bed to ask God for forgiveness?

Is he going to confess what he has done to his church since he is a man of God?

Is there somewhere in the Bible that says this is wrong?

I begin to imagine swimming furiously away from the shark, dodging him in holes he cannot fit through and darting among irregularly shaped rocks in the sea that his pointed snout cannot penetrate. I imagine myself churning up sand and burying myself beneath, hiding in my self-made tomb. *Did I do this? Does he think this is allowed because I told him I was being teased at school?*

I feel his warm, wet mouth on my breast. I am grossed out because I can feel his saliva running over my rib cage. *Why would he want to do this to me? I don't even have any breasts!*

I remember my childhood—*am I still a child?*—and walking hand in hand with my father and mother. We traveled throughout downtown Philadelphia, touring historic sites: the Benjamin Franklin National Memorial, the Liberty Bell, and sometimes we just went to the park. We took so many pictures. My mom and dad would take turns taking pictures of each other holding or sitting with me in various striking locations. One of my favorite sites was at a waterfront. My dad held me over his knee so that the picture would look as if I was sitting on the water. Before my mother took a picture, to try to get me to smile, she would ask, "Aliyana, what do you want to be when you grow up?" I would emphatically answer, while grinning wide, "I want to be a bird!" At that moment, she would take the photo while my father marveled at me as if I was the greatest creation God ever made. Well into the end of my days of elementary school, I would tell anyone who asked that I wanted to be a bird.

If only I could fly away right now.

◆ ◆ ◆

In the morning, I feel like crap. I must have a cold because my nose will not stop running. I wish it would run away from my face. Walking around looking like

Rudolph due to my fair skin meeting no-name toilet paper, I feel as if there is no skin left below my eyes and above my mouth. I have been sneezing, sniffling, and snorting since I woke up. I have the feeling today is going to be an awful day.

I leave the house at 6:22 a.m. to walk to the bus stop, only four homes away from our temporary home. It is amazing how many thoughts you can have during such a short walk.

Should pleasure be painful? I cannot help but replay the events from last night. I walk past daughters of affluent families who are not walking to the bus stop with me, but getting in vans to be driven to school by their fathers. I cannot help but wonder if they have ever experienced what I am feeling right now. Do they have men who come into their rooms? If so, do they have someone they can talk to about it? In an instant, I feel a hate in my heart. A hate for all of the cute teen girls who are riding to school with their fathers, living in these nice homes, wearing cool name-brand clothing. I hate them because I believe that should be me. That is what my life is supposed to be like, isn't it?

What am I supposed to say or do the next time I see Pastor Whitaker? Do I speak to him as if nothing has happened? Do I ask him, privately of course, why he is doing this? I know that what is happening between us is wrong. If it wasn't, then he would not wait until my sisters were asleep or my mother was away to commit these acts. Shamefully, I am not sure if I want these acts to end. I mean, no one else shows me attention. Hell, I don't even have a boyfriend, and probably never will, the way the kids tease me at school. I guess what I am feeling is, I like his attention. I would never show him that because of course that is wrong, but no one else notices me. No one else has told me I am pretty. No one else would kiss me the way he does.

Could it be that he really feels this way about me? What about my mom? Doesn't he like her that way too? I am confused. I have so many questions and no source to find the answers. Maybe he was not thinking last night, and maybe he won't do it again. Maybe.

The bus startles me as it arrives at the bus stop at 6:24.

❖ ❖ ❖

"Where do you think you're going?" my mother asked. She had overheard me talking to Layne about Grandma Marilyn's trip to Walt Disney World in Florida. Grandma Marilyn is very different from Grandma Ann. She is very stylish for an elderly woman, frequently ordering brightly colored ensembles from catalogs like Newport News. However, Grandma Marilyn is disabled after having a stroke in her late 40s. I never really saw her taking the best care of her health, smoking the strongest cigarettes that exist, Pall Malls, drinking plenty of Bacardi and eating infrequently. As a result of her stroke, Grandma Marilyn cannot use her left arm and right leg and has to wear a brace on both. The disability slows her down physically, but not mentally as she stays on the move.

Grandma Marilyn got the opportunity to go to Walt Disney World through the senior citizen center she frequents. The center was allowing all who were going to bring one person to assist them during the trip. Grandma Marilyn asked me because I regularly helped her around her apartment, and I was the oldest.

I tried to reply, "I'm just—"

"You take your sisters with you!" my mother shouted. "Do you think it's fair that you go and they stay in the house?" I felt as if the floor was falling from beneath me. I heard the laughter of my sisters playing in the next room. I love them so much and would have loved to take a photo with them standing beside Cinderella in front of a grand castle. But Grandma Marilyn said she could only take *one*. "If she can't take all of you, then none of ya'll asses going!"

I felt as if I just took a blow to the chest. What I considered a once-in-a-lifetime trip had just been snatched from me through no fault of my own. All I really wanted to do was help my Grandma Marilyn.

My mother continued to yell as I stood still, in silence, "You can't go places without your sisters! How does that make you look? Selfish, if you ask me."

At that moment, I figured I *was* selfish, along with every teenager in the world, because I don't see them toting their siblings around. Even if I could have taken them with me, I just felt that my mother would still have forbidden me to go. I cannot even go to a chaperoned birthday party. The offers continue—my aunt inviting me to Six Flags, a friend inviting me to the mall—but each time I have to turn them down.

It ended up that Grandma Marilyn went alone to a large theme park without any help, while I stayed at home with my sisters and cried, knowing I could have been having big fun. Grandma Marilyn thought she was helping by bringing me back a Disney World theme park picture book. I felt even worse.

1 YEAR LATER

Aliyana ❖ ❖ ❖

Until today, I have been sharing a room with my two sisters. Finally, today, I got to be alone, to be a teen: I got my own room. It was so unexpected. There is already much excitement flowing through the family because today is the first day we will walk through our new home, rebuilt from the ground up after the fire.

Pastor Whitaker drove down with the contractor to see us into our home. When we walk inside, I am amazed, taking in every sight and scent. I expect to smell the remnants of fire. Instead the house smells new, as if it has been recently taken out of a plastic package and placed on this cement slab. The setup is the same as before. The living room, bedrooms, and bathrooms are all in the same locations as they were in the old house. However, now there is brand-new furniture in every single room. The living room houses a burgundy and hunter green loveseat and sofa with a mahogany wooden table. There is a real television cabinet that not only has a space for the TV, but also has wide shelves for movies, music, books, and mementos. A shiny oak dining table and chairs with a matching hutch dominate the kitchen. Our refrigerator has an outer gadget that we push for ice and water without even opening it.

We proceed down the hall, as a family, and Pastor Whitaker points out our bedrooms. I feel a thrill, a sweet burning so deep in my heart that it is unstoppable by the outside world. I walk into a small room, almost small enough to be a storage room, containing all dark oak furnishings: a bed, a dresser with a large wall mirror, a small desk, and a tall chest.

There is one narrow window in the center of the room. There really isn't much space for anything to be added, but it is mine, all mine! I vow at this moment to keep it exceptionally clean, which I figure will please my mother and possibly even allow me to gain her favor. I also vow to keep everyone out of my room. It is my space, private and personal, that I am not going to allow anyone to invade.

Pastor Whitaker

At 8:30 p.m., I check to see if Layne and Anne are asleep. Layne is faintly snoring, while Anne makes no noise or movements. While it is as dark as midnight with the cloth window curtains closed, I can still faintly view the few dolls and clothing items strewn across the floor. I would think that in a brand new room, or house for that matter, they would try to be cleaner. They are just kids, so I guess this should be expected. I close the bedroom door as quietly as possible. Aliyana's room is next door. I lean my head against the door to find out if Aliyana could still be awake. Nothing. I slowly walk in.

This room, even with one shaded window, is pitch black. The smell of fruity lotion and hair products veil the room. I look to the left, in the dark, and wait for my eyes to adjust. I am careful not to move as the new wood under fresh, buzz-cut carpet could creak easily due to my heavy weight. I see the outline of Aliyana's body, heaving up and down slowly while she sleeps.

Aliyana seemed to have been bothered when she got off the bus today. She briskly walked up the driveway and rushed through the front door. When she saw me sitting on the couch, she looked blankly at me as if she did not know what to say or as if she was not expecting me to be there. I had to speak to her first, only to receive a "hi." I asked her if she was all right. She just nodded and went into her room and closed the door. I figured the kids in school were picking on her again.

Now, Aliyana seems to be at peace, which of course she should be in her own home. No one here is going to put her down or make her feel worthless. I want tomorrow to be a better day for her. I tiptoe into her bedroom and close the door behind me.

Aliyana

Uncle Dunk is one of the coolest people I know—almost as cool as Michael Jackson. They both have a way of "wooing" a crowd, getting the groupies to fall in love with them. Michael Jackson's groupies are all around the world, and he mostly woos through his attractiveness and his fierce, meticulous dance moves. Uncle Dunk woos through his playful personality. His groupies are all of the youth in our family.

Uncle Dunk stands over 6 feet tall with arm muscles so large they are always bulging through his shirtsleeves. He will not be caught without a baseball cap of some sort sitting over his long, Jheri curled hair. He loves to tell jokes. Most of his jokes are funny unless you are the butt of them. I never am. As a matter of fact, he always tells jokes to keep me laughing and smiling. I used to think he felt sorry for me because someone was always picking on me. I have come to realize that he genuinely cares about me. For some odd reason, I also think he firmly believes that I am some type of prodigy who will overcome the country life and become something big, something wonderful—or at least that is how he makes me feel.

Every kid in our family loves him. He is like the ultimate mentor, always showing up when something is going wrong and willing to listen to us vent and vent... and vent. I always feel so guilty for consuming so much of his time with miserable stories that are beyond his control. No problem for Uncle Dunk, though; he not only listens but also gives great advice. I get so excited, along with my sisters, my cousins, and his son, to see him. At this point, I feel as if it is life or death.

I know that I must talk to someone about what is going on between Pastor Whitaker and me. I cannot even count at this point how many times he has come into my bedroom, after putting my sisters to bed, and stayed until my mother returns home from work. The things that he does, that I continuously recall over and over again, as if there is nothing else in the world to think of, I know have to be wrong. In fact, I know they are wrong, but I just need someone to tell me how to make it all stop. Of course I cannot tell my mother, as I know it will hurt, seeing that he sleeps in her bedroom after leaving my room. I am too embarrassed to tell my best friend at school. I sure as heck am not going to tell anyone who has a big mouth. I definitely am not going to tell my father, who would quickly consider ending Pastor Whitaker's life without much thought. I figure the safest person for me to talk to would be Uncle Dunk.

"Hey Uncle Dunk! How are you?" I say as I run up to him and give him a hug with both arms. He always pats my back as I squeeze him.

"I'm good. The question is how are *you* doing, squeezing me like you are crazy," he says, chuckling.

"Guess what?"

"What's that?"

"I got a summer job!" I am too excited to tell him the details. As soon as I release the good news, my mood quickly changes as I remember what I really need to talk to him about. Uncle Dunk proceeds to walk into Grandma Ann's house. Before he fully opens the door, I blurt out, "Are you coming back outside? I need to talk to you."

"Yeah, let me just get some water and check on my boy. I'll come right out."

The five minutes that it takes Uncle Dunk to greet his parents and son feel like five days to me. My mind wrestles with what to say. Yes, I have always been able to talk to Uncle Dunk, but I have mostly shared with him my difficulties in school and with my mom, my future goals and dreams and how to obtain them, and our shared love of Michael Jackson. No matter what the topic of conversation, I always feel encouraged and inspired when our conversations finish. I am not too sure if I will obtain the same result after this conversation.

My thoughts are broken by the sound of laughter. Between his jokes, exposing the children to video games, and listening and dancing to music, Uncle Dunk loves to have fun. I figure he is playing around with his son. At this moment, jealousy surges through me. I have to admit, seeing other children or teens enjoying time with their parents makes me so angry. I often question God about why I cannot have this with my mother. Sometimes, after praying and reading my New Testament Gideon Bible, I feel empowered enough to believe that if I try one more time to talk to her, our relationship will change. I want to pour my heart out to her, tell her how kids tease her first-born child in school, how her baby so badly wants a perm, and advice on how to deal with a terrible crush that involves me liking a boy at school who practically does not even know that I exist. With my dad, I always have fun, but the brief time that we have to spend with him during our bi-weekly visitations, rudely cut short by my mom, makes my heart ache.

"OK, Aliyana, what's up, girl?" Uncle Dunk greets me again walking down the steps. I love the fact that he talks to me like a friend, an adult. "What has your mother done now?"

"She didn't do anything outside of the norm," I chuckle, still trying to figure out how to pose the information to my uncle that currently only two people have knowledge of.

"I haven't really said much to Mommy lately, so I guess that is why we have not really had any issues. I wanted to talk to you about my friend in school."

"Ok..." he says, waiting for me to continue.

"I got a summer job! I will be working as a secretary for a middle school," I continue our conversation from a few minutes ago.

"That is great! You are doing big things, girl. Now, when you start working, make sure you save some of your money. Even if it is only 10 dollars every time you get paid. OK?"

"I will try. You know, Mommy said that when I start working I have to help pay the bills, so I am not sure how much she will let me keep."

"I will talk to her about that, because you need to be saving, or at least being taught how to."

I nod, agreeing with my uncle, and I decide to just throw out to him what I really want to discuss. "So I have this friend. She is really nice to everybody and does well in school."

"Is this your friend whose dad is a pastor of a church?" he asks.

"Oh, yeah," I lie. "She told me that she is in a relationship with an older man. They even have sex. He is like 40 or something—well, he is much older than her."

"How old is she?" Uncle Dunk asks, sounding disturbed.

"She is the same age as me. So is that wrong? She asked me at lunch yesterday."

"Do her parents know?" Uncle Dunk has a habit of asking many questions before getting to the advice part that I so eagerly want to hear.

"No, she kind of feels the same way about her mom that I feel about mine. She can't talk to her."

Uncle Dunk looks at me, still disturbed. I wonder if he realizes that I am talking about myself.

"You do know that what they are doing is illegal. She is a minor. The man who is sleeping with her can go to jail."

He can? I had not even considered Pastor Whitaker going to jail. My mother would probably really hate me if I got the man that she is so close to locked up.

"She better end it if she knows what is good for her," he says.

I get that message loud and clear.

Aliyana

Tonight is different and unbelievably painful. I tried to pretend that I was asleep. I felt him poking around my private area with his own as he has done many times in the past. However, after months of attempts and asking me why I didn't let him "in," Pastor Whitaker penetrated me. Previously, and as recently as yesterday, it was only petting, rubbing, touching and pretending. Tonight, I could not pretend that I was asleep. I gasp when he enters me. I question why people enjoy this miserable act currently occurring between the two of us. I have a conversation with God, asking Him why would one of His great servants do this to me. If this was what sex feels like, I never, ever want to feel this again.

I wake up feeling like the weight of the world was dumped on my shoulders and between my legs. I moved my leg to turn on my side and face the wall so that I would not have to look anyone in the eye if they walked into my room. For some reason, my bed sheets feel wet. I look underneath the covers, hesitantly and afraid of what I would see. Blood without cramps—I didn't even think it was possible since the cramps always warn me of my visit from Lady Period. It seems strange, but I get up out of the bed so that I can clean myself up. Aside from the throbbing and burning between my legs and all of the confusion from last night swimming around in my mind, I felt fine. While using the bathroom, the stinging sensation of urinating made me want to flush myself down the toilet. I hurriedly put on a maxi pad, lay a towel over the surprisingly small amount of blood in my bed and lay back down to sleep until someone comes into my room to force me to get up. Before falling asleep, I recount last night and wonder if how I am feeling is the definition of depression.

I get out of the bed only twice today to eat junk food—Swiss Cake Rolls. I had no meat, no vegetables, no real meal. I lay back down for bed around 8:00 p.m. I find it odd that after finding blood on my sheets this morning that I had none on my maxi pads all day. Maybe it is coming and the blood was a warning? I am not sure about anything seeing that I could not concentrate on anything except the fact that I felt that I cheated on my mother with our cousin. How in the world was I to explain this to her if she ever found out? How in the heck would I explain this to God before entering heaven? I feel now that my destiny is hell, and I am on a fast train to this revolting destination.

I am sick of waking up! I got up first about two hours ago to use the bathroom. Feeling as if my bladder would explode, I sit on the toilet only to release a small amount of urine. Within the past two hours, I have had the feeling of having to use the bathroom about eight times. The distressing part is that I did not go to the bathroom each of these times. At night, because of how small our home is, every time I get up, or anyone for that matter, it is easily heard. I could not justify going to the bathroom that many times within a two-hour period if my mom asked. What I realized, however, is that I did not really have to go. I had an overwhelming feeling to urinate, but nothing would come out when I actually tried to. When I did, very, very little would trickle out like a tease. After the first two bathroom visits, I went to the bathroom in a Styrofoam cup I found after scurrying in my closet for something to relieve myself in. I wonder if Pastor Whitaker gave me some type of disease.

I return home from a carnival with Uncle Dunk. This carnival was the most fun I have ever had besides singing and dancing to Michael Jackson in the back of my grandmother's house by myself or reading a good book. Uncle Dunk had to work, assisting with the maintenance of machinery used at the carnival. I volunteered to help him, knowing good and well that I could not lift nor fix anything electronic. The carnival took place during the time that Mommy had to work, so I did not necessarily have to ask if I could go, and I was delighted to not have my sisters tagging along behind me. Instead, my uncle allowed me to help his co-workers with entertaining the children and playing games. I had more fun being a volunteer than a participant.

The hour long ride home was even better, as once again I had Uncle Dunk all to myself to chat about the things that I feel that I cannot deal with alone. He gave me advice on dealing with Mommy, "Don't talk back to her. Just keep doing well in school and eventually you can get out of her house and live a good life. You only have one mother, and you should love her, but like I've said before... she is my sister, and I know what she is capable of. Don't let it get to you." He talked to me about school, "I wish I had some of the opportunities that you have in school. Plus, you are smart, Aliyana. All you need to do right now is focus on school. You are beautiful too? That is a great combination, and you are going to be something great when you get older." I wondered if he would bring up my "friend" that I talked to him about the other day. He didn't.

Sadie Mae

That bastard! Men who prey on children ought to have their balls cut off and thrown to the dogs. I can't stand to see a man taking advantage of a female. I went through that crap with Richard. I sure as hell am not going to sit back and let my brother do that crap to Aliyana.

First of all, I did not tell him that he had permission to take Aliyana to that carnival. I am her mother—he is to get my permission first. I had to find out from my mother that he took my child away from where I left her. I don't know why my mother let Aliyana leave her house, but you know people like to take advantage of the elderly. Aliyana knew better than to leave. Then, here she comes asking me for some maxi pads! Why is she on her period so early? I know when it is supposed to start, and it is early. What did my brother do to her to make her period come on? I just don't understand. I ask Aliyana about it, and she wants to defend him? My brother ain't worth nothing! He did something to her, made her period come on, and she wants to act like I have wronged her by asking about it. Well, if she wants to go around and allow strange men to touch her and be promiscuous that is on her, but she is not going to live in my house carrying out this poor behavior. I did not teach this to her!

Aliyana

There are times when I love to receive gifts. I get most of them from my friends at school for my birthday or some random BFF gift. These small tokens of appreciation: Calgon bath sets, spaghetti strapped tank tops and note card sets, meant more to me than my friends would ever know. I treasured the gifts because they meant that someone cared about and thought of me. Shucks, a simple hug, silly song or homemade card was all I needed to be elated about being alive another year. However, some gifts are not worth taking.

In the past year of being forced to sleep with the enemy, which Pastor Whitaker was making a habit of on Monday and Tuesday nights since my mother's shift always ended at 9 p.m., I have received more than enough gifts from a grown man. Sometimes I figure my mom will question me on the large amount of items that I have received, while my sisters receive barely anything. I have gotten clothes, name brand sneakers, costume jewelry, hair products and other small trinkets, but all on the expensive side—the things that my mother would not ever purchase for me.

Next week will be my 16th birthday. I expect to have a great day at school, where I feel the safest and most loved, where my friends will sing to me and fill my book bag with more body wash sets. I am not expecting any gifts at home, except from Pastor Whitaker. He has already told me that he has something "special" for me. He considers everything that he has given me to be special. I can consider them to be as fake and phony as his license to pastor a church.

Pastor Whitaker, as much as he takes my side and defends me when Mommy is putting me down or yelling at me, as much as he says that I can talk to him about anything and that nothing will separate us, causes me much more pain and grief than he can imagine.

My Uncle Dunk is being blamed for something that Pastor Whitaker is doing to me. First of all, I did not know that my period started because of sex. And was it really my period? I sure wish I could talk to a female about this stuff because I just don't get it. I thought Lady Period just visited monthly? Now, I am really confused. Anyways, my mother comes into my room two days after the carnival ranting about how much of a bastard my uncle is and how he is going to hell if he did anything to me. She questioned me and questioned me, as if she was trying to get me to admit that Uncle Dunk did something wrong. As much as I wanted to yell out, "It is not Uncle Dunk, dummy, it's your cousin!" I didn't. I just tell her over and over, "No" to each of her questions. Did he touch me? Did he do anything he wasn't supposed to do with me? Did I ask her permission to go to the carnival? Was I alone with him at the park? It is crazy that her suspicions are against my uncle and not the man that she leaves me alone with at least twice a week. If Lady Period visited me this month as a result of sex, it was the man buying me gifts who caused it. Why couldn't Mommy see this?

Pastor Whitaker

I continue to show Aliyana and her mother how much I love and respect them. I figure that Aliyana does not like that I sleep in the bedroom with her mother, but I am not sleeping with her the same way. Sadie Mae is too reserved, especially after overcoming such a horrible marriage. She is paranoid about everything, which severely interferes with any lovemaking that we could have. This is why I appreciate Aliyana so much. She allows me to be free with her body and explore. She does not reject me nor fight back. Heck, she doesn't even move. Her body, unknown to men except by me, is a fairground of limitless activities. It was hard to get through to her at first, as she was reserved and timid, but eventually she opened up, I think. Aliyana may just go through the motions because she has so much to learn. I mean, she is only 15, until next week anyways.

As I put my robe over my cocoa butter drenched skin, I think about her birthday. At 16 years old, legally, a teen can make a lot of decisions. At this age they can drive, decide whether or not they want to drop out of school, emancipate themselves, and even give consent to consensual sex. I cannot wait for the opportunity to have more freedom with Aliyana. I have told her that I would like to marry her when she is old enough, but I don't believe this would really happen. Her mother would be devastated, and her family would not understand. For some reason, I don't get the feeling that she wants to marry me, but I figure this is due to her being naive and unsure of her future, let alone *our* future. I must keep reassuring her that I will always be in her corner so that we can continue to share our love for years to come.

It's 8:33 p.m. when I check to see if Anne and Layne are asleep. After confirming so, I go into Aliyana's room and close the door. I still have about an hour before her mother is due to arrive home from work. Once again, Aliyana is asleep already. I am sure I will be able to easily wake her with arousal. I pull the covers from over her head. I have learned how to maneuver in her room without being able to see. I begin to feel around on her body to determine what she is wearing, while I imagine her wearing something entirely different. No need for imagining tonight, however. She has on only a t-shirt and panties—more arousing than the imaginations of lingerie. I feel her breasts, small but supple. I must have been too rough because Aliyana stirs and attempts to turn on her side, only to do so partially. I slowly walk around to the end of her bed and pull the covers down to her ankles.

I begin to pull her underwear down, and I only get them to her knees before I hear what sounds like a car door slam from outside. I check the glow in the dark hands of my watch, knowing that an hour could not have passed that quickly. I was really taking my time because I did not even expect a half hour to pass. Sure enough, it was only minutes after 9 p.m. That cannot be Sadie Mae that I hear outside. It is too early. Seconds later, I hear the car horn of the door being locked. I quickly throw the covers back over Aliyana, neglecting to pull her panties up again, tie up my robe, which I allow to hang open in the dark with Aliyana, and walk out, closing the door to her room. I am only one footstep down the hall before I realize that Sadie Mae is facing me.

Sadie Mae

I am so thankful to have gotten off early tonight because my feet are killing me. I was sure that C.J. would be glad to see me, but I am not too sure when I see his face after walking into the house. He has on only a robe and looks troubled instead of pleased to see me. He usually smells clean and fragrant with the scent of some type of department store cologne, but tonight he had an overwhelming smell of cocoa butter. What in the world was he doing? I did not want to even consider what he was doing.

Pastor Whitaker

"I was relaxing, Sadie Mae, good grief. You know I had a long drive here yesterday; I am only trying to relax. I was laying in your room and just came out for something to drink, that's all," I respond to her question of why I was only in a robe in the dark. I cannot help but wonder if she saw what room I came out of and if she knows that I was with Aliyana.

"I mean, I am just asking. You don't usually sit around in a robe, and that is why I asked what you were doing."

"So you tell me, what do you think I was doing, Sadie Mae?" I attempt to say passively. I really did not want to hear her answer to this question.

"C.J., I just asked. I am tired, and I don't want to argue. Did you eat? You want me to make something for you to eat?"

"That would be nice," I say.

Aliyana

Oh my God, really?! The moment that he could have been caught, that all of this sex would have ended, ends with him having a meal fixed for him by my mother? She is not going to ask him why he is in her house naked with her three daughters asleep in their rooms? Is she crazy?!! I retreat into a despairing sleep, made even more difficult with the bitter solace of silent, hot tears streaming down my face and onto my pillow.

epilogue

Without suitable protection and safety, most youth feel abortive. A meal protects my physical health, but what about my mental health? Just say an encouraging word. Clothing helps my body withstand the hot and cold weather conditions, but my parents still have to protect and cover me and my body even when I take my clothing off. The skin I am in and the mind within it needs a constant defense.

Once when my parents were still together, my dad attempted to teach me how to ride my bicycle without the training wheels. This was such a troubling issue for me because I could not fathom riding my bike without those two additional petite wheels hanging off the side of my bike like the wings of an airplane. The pink training wheels were a safety precaution for me, the same way a floating device was when we went to the beach. There was no way I would jump in the water without my life jacket; no way I am riding without my training wheels.

My dad, with an enthusiastic and unusually patient attitude, encouraged me to get on my bike like I normally would, and he would guard me by holding on. With reluctance and some anxiety, I sit on the seat, which is still smooth and white with pink strawberries floating on the surface. I took a moment to take pride in the fact that after all of this time and much riding, I took great care of my bike. The only visible wear and tear was on the outer circles of the front and back tires, and my training wheels, now removed and thrown to the side, in the grass.

Looking at my training wheels, delicate yet thrown inside growing weeds, somehow did not feel right. This was all too soon. It was not time for them to be buried beneath a mound of hardware in the garage. Seeing them laying in solace, as if they were in preparation for a funeral, made me feel as if I lost something that I could never get back. I needed those wheels.

I slide onto the bike seat, which seemed so much higher than before without the training wheels. My heart begins to race, but I looked back to find my father holding on to the edge of one handlebar and my seat. He began to push the bike while telling me to pedal. At first I was unstable and off balance, probably due to the fact that we were still on the gravel in the driveway. My dad guides me onto the street, an intimidating, yet smoother ride.

My dad was yelling while holding on to the bike, "Keep pedaling, Aliyana" and "You're doing good, Aliyana" until I felt comfortable enough to keep pedaling without looking back. In fact, he practically forbade it. Whenever my neck turned slightly to see if he was still there, he would emphatically scream, "Don't look back!" When his cheerleading seemed to have trailed off, I did just what he told me not to do: I looked back.

It was a rollercoaster without the theme park. I leaned, swerved, tumbled and fell knee first onto the hot pavement. The scene resembled a catastrophic car accident where the car is on one side of the road and the body of the victim is on the opposite. I look up, not even realizing I was hurt. As my dad ran closer—I did not know he was that far away—I began to feel an intense throbbing in what seemed to be my entire leg. I began to scream and cry simultaneously.

The next day, when it finally didn't hurt to stretch my leg out completely, I began to examine what would become a lifelong scar. A scab, profusely draining my blood yesterday yet a hard clot today, sat as high as a soap bubble on a child's nose. In the shape of Africa, my scab would serve as a reminder as long as I could see it that I messed up. I stared at it in awe, thinking if only I didn't look back.

Later, and I don't know why, I took pleasure in picking my scab. Don't get me wrong, I can't stand the sight of the brownish, black and crusty discharge that has formed to heal my wound. However, I get such a thrill, maybe even a release, from slowly and carefully pulling back the edges of the sore. As if I was a doctor carefully performing a surgery, I picked the pieces of the scab off and examined the area that used to be the crust of my skin. I wondered and questioned why I was doing this to myself, but I continued.

The scab was dominating my mind, controlling me and causing me to do what I didn't want to. Once I finished prepping the edges, I peeled the remainder of the scab, even though it hurt, until it was completely off. I sat on the floor of the living room and looked at the reopened wound on my right knee, rubbing the area around it to stop the stinging sensation. What is left behind after my personal, artificial surgery is a thick, burgundy, oozing mixture of my cells—blood. As I tried to tame the blood and keep it from dripping onto the carpet, my mother walked out of her bedroom.

"Aliyana, what the hell are you doing?" she screamed.

"I was just—"

"You know what, that's alright. It's your body and you wanna mark it all up and have it all looking black and ugly, that's on you! I ain't the one that's gotta walk around looking like that! It is you who have to live with that scar. Now, go clean that mess up before you mess up my rug!" I began to question if my mother even cared that I was hurt. She seemed to be much more concerned about the rug.

I proceeded to limp into the bathroom, unnecessarily holding my leg with a torn piece of napkin covering the wound. When I passed the window, I saw my dad carrying my limp wheels in his hands, preparing them for the funeral of a long life of storage, maybe even trash.

Although I still did not know how to ride my bike without the training wheels, I learned lessons from this experience. First, I need to do whatever I can to keep my scabs, my protective coverings, over my blood. Second, when a man I trust stands directly beside me, encouraging me that he is right there, I can still fall. Finally, no matter what, do not ever look back.

Who empowers her community through mentoring girls, uplifting abuse survivors and blogging about looking and feeling great while living life on purpose?

LaQuisha Hall, the "Unbothered Queen" of Confidence, goes far beyond what is expected of her. There was a time in LaQuisha's life where she was not confident in much. She struggled through low self-esteem due to being naturally thin, witnessed domestic violence as a child and was sexually abused by clergy as a teen. Now an international advocate for herself and others, LaQuisha actively works to empower women and youth to overcome catastrophe through Coutured Confidence.

LaQuisha is a force to be reckoned with in communities. She is an award-winning community service leader, winning regional, state and national pageant titles including Mrs. Essence 2013. She founded the SheRose Awards to give a platform to abuse survivors to share their own stories. Beginning her skills in mentoring at age 16, she also spends hours locally and abroad mentoring via her nonprofit program, Queendom T.E.A. (The Etiquette Academy), committed to encouraging and teaching teen girls about personal safety, feminine etiquette and positive self-esteem.

She is the author of a self-esteem journal for young girls, Positively Bodyful, and the coauthor of additional books. LaQuisha also enjoys keeping her look fresh while inspiring others as the natural hair and fashion guru behind Corner Curl Girl.

Her "survive, then conquer" philosophy teaches communities to not only overcome catastrophe, but to support others in doing the same. LaQuisha has empowered others to empower others for over a decade and has no plans of stopping!

WE WANT TO HEAR FROM YOU!!!

If this book has made a difference in your life LaQuisha would be delighted to hear about it.
Leave a review on Amazon.com!

BOOK LAQUISHA TO SPEAK AT YOUR NEXT EVENT!

Send an email to: booking@publishyourgift.com

Learn more about LaQuisha at:
www.LaQuishaHall.com

FOLLOW LAQUISHA ON SOCIAL MEDIA

 laquishahall laquisha_hall

---

"EMPOWERING YOU TO IMPACT GENERATIONS"
WWW.PUBLISHYOURGIFT.COM

www.ingramcontent.com/pod-product-compliance
Lightning Source LLC
Chambersburg PA
CBHW070637170726
48291CB00003B/1049